ALSO BY WILLIAM F. WELD

Mackerel by Moonlight

BIG
UGLY

A Novel

WILLIAM F. WELD

SIMON & SCHUSTER

SIMON & SCHUSTER
Rockefeller Center
1230 Avenue of the Americas
New York, NY 10020

This book is a work of fiction. Names, characters,
places, and incidents either are products of the
author's imagination or are used fictitiously. Any
resemblance to actual events or locales or persons,
living or dead, is entirely coincidental.

Copyright © 1999 by William F. Weld
SIMON & SCHUSTER and colophon are
registered trademarks of Simon & Schuster, Inc.
Designed by Edith Fowler
Manufactured in the United States of America

10 9 8 7 6 5 4 3 2 1

Library of Congress Cataloging-in-Publication Data

Weld, William F.
  Big Ugly : a novel / William F. Weld.
    p.   cm.
  I. Title.
PS3573.E4547B5   1999
813'.54—dc21   99-41480
                    CIP
ISBN 0-684-85347-7

To Ethel

BIG UGLY

WASHINGTON sure is a funny town.

I was brimful of confidence when I arrived from Boston in January 1999. I was thirty-five years old, and had just knocked off a three-term Republican U.S. senator to help my party re-take the majority. Pretty heady stuff.

Better yet, I had already proved myself adept at political high-wire acts. You know how sometimes they say, everybody's got something to hide? Let me tell you, I came with a closetful of that stuff, some from my early days as a prosecutor in New York, and some much more recent, in New England. I had successfully kept a lid on all of it through two nasty and high-profile campaigns for elected office, for all the marbles. Not bad.

The only problem, as soon as I hit Washington, D.C., I lose my footing. Suddenly, my life is being dominated by two senators I've never met before, Harlan "Happy" Gilliam of Texas and Anson Vivian from the coal country of West Virginia, and I'm making one false move after another, and in six months, I'm further in over my head than I've ever been, right back in the soup. This is the story of those six months.

Gilliam and Vivian were both actually trying to help me, and got me into serious trouble in different ways. It took the lady from Florida to extricate me, and believe me, she wasn't setting out to do me any favors, it just worked out that way.

At the end of the day, I had pretty well squared all my accounts, but it took some doing. It's just a funny town, is all. Takes a little getting used to.

Part One

THE FIRST SINKHOLE was dug for me by Happy Gilliam, the chairman of the Democratic Senatorial Campaign Committee.

I never should have laughed at what Happy said. He didn't intend it as a joke, but it was so politically incorrect, it just tickled my funny bone.

"I live for the fund-raising, frankly," was what he said. "It's my favorite part of the job. In fact, it's the only part of the job I like."

I was the only member of the caucus who laughed. Maybe that should have told me something.

Gilliam had to know if these words were repeated to the media by any of the dozen senators present, they could have a major negative impact on his presidential campaign. Yet he was not worried about leaks, and he was right. The necessity for constant fund-raising made every member of the Senate kith and kin. We were all, every one of us, Democrat and Republican, parties to a vast conspiracy against the laity, more particularly against donors, and most particularly of all against donors who were also lobbyists.

So Happy Gilliam, part Sioux and part millionaire, one-time national trapshooting champion, now the people's champion from the Texas panhandle, spoke freely: "When I was in private practice, I got to have truck with smart, rich, well-educated folk all day long. Now—whew!" He mopped his huge, handsome eyebrows. "Now I can't wait for the fund-raisers. Come on six o'clock, bye-bye Girl Scouts, hello smoked salmon and bubbly, and *hello there*, Miss Becky, that's sure a lovely name tag you have on there! Right there."

My laughter echoed off the walls of the caucus room. I looked up at the paintings of two former chairmen of the Campaign Committee. They were stern, disapproving. I looked around the big oak table at the Democratic members, all veterans except for me and "Binky" Brownswall from Nebraska. Two or three thin smiles. No one else laughed.

I couldn't figure out why. Gilliam had a point, and it was funny. There are never any frowny faces at fund-raising events, not at breakfast, not at lunch, and not at cocktails. Everyone there is highly paid, except for the elected officials. These events are our taste of flying first class. We can't take it in salary, so we take it in kind. The press is rigorously excluded; all the stars are in alignment for a full, free, and frank exchange of views.

Except, that's what never happens. What does happen is the lobbyists present their views, and the senators listen. And eat. Thoughtfully. And nod. It doesn't matter if your mouth is full of smoked salmon and caviar, because the last thing anyone wants or expects is for you to say anything. Or, worse, ask a question. If there's one thing you don't ask at fund-raisers, Gilliam told me early on, it's questions.

With a couple of campaigns behind me, I had internalized that the fund-raising operation never sleeps, not even between elections that are six years apart. But even I, big-city cosmopolitan Terrence Mullally, was not prepared for the pace. I had almost six years to go before my reelect, and I was doing eight events a week.

In April 1999, I had been in Washington three months. I was perched on the arm of a chintz chair in my inner office in the Hart Senate Office Building, talking alone with Lanny Green, my brilliant boy wonder chief of staff.

"Make hay while the sun shines," Lanny advised me. Lanny is a twenty-six-year-old veteran. Notice: not a twenty-six-*year* veteran. He seems to know Washington cold. He's actually from the District, born here, but Southeast, not Northwest. His father was a hardworking Mexican, had a lousy job with the railroad, raised Lanny attentively. His mother drifted away early—drugs—but Lanny's dad stuck his mother's name on him on the theory it was more "acceptable." Father's surname was "Analfabetismo," or something. Guy was a saint. Lanny never talks about him. Or his mother.

"How come the sun is shining? I'm on lousy committees with no influence, and I'm the most junior member of the club."

Lanny took this in stride. His expression didn't change. Maybe his eyes narrowed a bit. Lanny's a good-looking guy, though he has no size to him. Light brown hair cut short—stops at the top of the ears, no sideburns. He wears tweed herringbone jackets, though he's the least tweedy person I know. Pays no attention to grooming. Ridiculous floppy Hush Puppies that he never takes off. Lanny would never be accepted as a principal in any profession, just as an aide. He doesn't care. He lives inside his head. Hazel eyes, not distinguished. He makes them dull, no intelligence showing. Protective coloration, not unknown in the animal kingdom.

"Point taken as to Ethics and Judiciary, Boss, but while you may think Agriculture is a jerkwater committee because your stupid state—excuse me, *our* stupid state—doesn't have any plant life, the rest of this glorious rich-soil country we live in views it as the goddamn hot corner. You think the soybean and sugar people are knocking down our doors to raise money for you because they want to talk about the Massachusetts soybean industry? Not in Worcester, not in New Bedford, not in Ripton, trust me. Or maybe your views about desirable qualifications for federal judges? Better pack a lunch."

"I thought they wanted to ask me what I really think about ethics. I could give them an earful of Aristotle . . ."

"That would go over big. You'll get your chance, anyway, at the event at the Humphrey Center on Thursday. It's all for you, and you alone."

"Who's coming?"

"Soybeans, corn, wheat, sugar—cane and beet—some garden veggies. Those last actually *do* care about immigration, and they're on the right side of the issue—namely, liberal—for the wrong reason—namely, exploitation of migrant labor. I love it." Lanny and I shared a well-developed sense of the absurd.

"Any human beings?"

"Depends what you call Happy Gilliam."

"Why the hell is he coming?" I shouldn't tell this, but I had been rather enjoying the idea of my very own party, where I would be the only object of flattery and attention, and wouldn't even have to perform.

Lanny put his face close to mine. "Only one reason, Boss," he whispered. "Nobody else will come without him."

"Oh. Why didn't you say so? So." I shrugged to show I didn't care.

■

Most of the lobbyists in attendance at the Hubert Horatio Humphrey Center on Thursday, April 8, had one thing in common. Can you guess?

They had breathtaking legs.

Happy Gilliam, known to be a ladies' man, had arrived early and was not making much of an effort to look anyone in the eye.

I drew Lanny to the far side of the gigantic ice sculpture depicting dolphins, mermaids, and a big man with horns and a trident. "I forget," I said. "Is this about money or sex? I thought it was about money."

"It is, Boss, the micros are just to get your attention. Think of it as a mnemonic aid."

"Funny, vegetables are not what I think of when—"

"Vegetables? Who said anything about vegetables? 'Hush yoah mouf,' " he hissed in imitation of Happy Gilliam. " 'Weah talkin' prass spoats, son, prass spoats puren' simple.' "

I lowered my head. "What?"

"Price supports. Republican orthodoxy hates them. These

people are not displeased to see the Dems back on top. You're against Republican orthodoxy, remember? That stick-in-the-mud Harold Dellenbach. You hated him, remember? And you did the country and these people a favor by beating him, don't ever forget. *Hsst,* here they come."

A row of legs advanced on us, precision-marching. Why how dee-lighted I was to see each and every one of them, I understood they had already been most generous and I was highly appreciative, no I'd not yet had an opportunity to review *in detail* the administration's proposal to do away with price supports entirely, it had not in point of fact come up in my campaign so I certainly had an *open mind* on the issue . . .

These were all code words. They meant, give me more money. The Rockettes understood this. The oldest among them—and if she was over thirty, I'm Mahatma Gandhi—took one step toward me and spoke quickly, distinctly: "Senator, I'm Sarah Blakeslee. The stakes for our industry are actually higher than you might imagine. Adoption of the Brinker bill"—she evidently knew I was not a fan of President Brinker—"would be absolutely devastating to the millions of American families who depend on us. Many of them"—she smiled cunningly without missing a beat—"many of them low-income families, especially immigrant families from south of the Border, with no other means of support for their children."

Thanks to you, I thought. Or did I say that? I quickly scanned their faces. No, I hadn't said it. Better start paying more attention, though. God, you're never safe. I put down my glass of champagne, still full.

She had me pegged as a big-time liberal because of where I came from. She couldn't possibly know about Lanny's father, or how close I was to Lanny. Or could she? She was not looking at Lanny or including him in the conversation—but that's how a class act would play it. When you're doing someone's friend a favor, you don't rub it in while they're both present. That way you preserve everybody's pride. And deniability.

"We expect the vote in the committee to be relatively close, but in all likelihood favorable." Why was she telling me she didn't need my vote? Did I drink that champagne? No, those were shrimp. Gah!

"The problem, for us and those we employ, including those of modest means, is that as soon as the committee's recommendation reaches the floor, there will be no shortage of demagogues, there will be no shortage of columnists or editorial writers, to bellow that the committee is a pawn of special interests, that the recommendation was bought and paid for, and that the matter must be viewed as though the committee had never held a hearing, or called a witness."

"But I don't have any of your products in my state."

"Precisely my point, Senator. We don't need more support from the tobacco states. We don't need more support from the farm belt. They'll be laughed out of town by the national media. We need an *honest broker*, a person of recognized intelligence and integrity who comes to these issues, these problems, with a fresh eye. We need credibility on our issues, Senator. You've got it."

I chuckled. "Credibility, but no background," I observed.

"Oh, we can get y'all the background," was the enthusiastic suggestion from a junior Rockette, the only one falling out of the top of her dress as well as the bottom. The lead negotiator wheeled on her, and I was glad I couldn't see her expression, because whatever it was, the junior Rockette shut her mouth and shrank right back into her dress.

Rockette in Chief turned to me with a businesslike smile. She walked to the side, with Gilliam in tow. I saw I was to follow, and did so.

"We are prepared to be generous," she said.

"How do you know where I'm going to come out?"

"We don't. We just . . . we're prepared to be generous." She looked up at Gilliam's massive head. As the Lord is my witness, he patted her behind. "I can vouch for that," he said. This surprised me. The lady did not look or act like a bimbo. Her clothes were Talbot's all the way, her face showed character. And I *was* looking at her face.

She turned back to me. Her expression was pleasant, her

voice inaudible beyond our group of three. "Tonight has raised fifty thousand dollars so far," she said briskly. "If it would not *offend* you to make an in-depth and *good faith* study of our issues, with a view to becoming a disinterested champion if, and only if, you should be persuaded of the merits of our cause . . . we will raise another three hundred seventy-five thousand."

This was a mood-changer. I glanced at Gilliam, who could not have failed to hear. He was looking into the middle distance. His expression was 100 percent approval.

"Sounds reasonable," I said, forgetting to pause thoughtfully first. I barely resisted the temptation to pluck at my chin, but it would've been too late anyway. They could see the hook coming right out through my gill plate.

I drew Gilliam aside before it was time to go. We bowed our heads in conversation—a sign no one was to join us.

"Is this real, Happy? Do they honestly think there's a snowball's chance in hell the administration will follow through with that bill? It's just not like them. That Ohio mafia is damn near corrupt wherever big business is concerned, near as I can tell, and agriculture is big business."

Senator Gilliam seemed troubled by this. His voice dropped to a whisper.

"Yes, it is real, and they are worried. If it were merely a question of reaching, of persuading, President Brinker and his staff, that would be one thing. But that cowgirl from Florida is using the national press to push the bill, and that makes it difficult for the president. Cuts into his flexibility."

The cowgirl reference was to Martha Holloway, the vice president of the United States, like Gilliam an expert shot. She had been a maverick one-term governor of Florida, and had been handpicked for the ticket to deliver two things: women's votes, and the state of Florida. As usual, she had gone two for two. Actually, she usually went twenty-five for twenty-five.

"I knew she had a save-the-Everglades bill, but what does she care about the rest of this stuff? I thought she just hated sugarcane."

"She's looking for issues for 2000; she doesn't really care."

"So you're with the camp that says Myron Brinker won't run again?"

"I don't know. It's a free country, and he's sixty-five."

"Sixty-six," I corrected him.

"Whatever," said Gilliam, and walked off in the direction of Miss Blakeslee's well-cut pink suit. I let him go alone.

■

My PROSECUTORIAL INSTINCTS led me to shake hands with every single Rockette and other hanger-on in the room before leaving, looking each one in the eye and repeating their name out loud. *If you're going to be receiving a lot of money in contributions, you better know or have met a lot of people.* Otherwise, some bored and trigger-happy assistant U.S. attorney might start asking a lot of dumb questions. Like, where did all this money come from and what was it for? Okay, so maybe not so dumb, really.

Having already begun work on my cover story, I was feeling well pleased with myself as Lanny and I left the veggies behind and jaywalked across Louisiana Avenue to meet my bride at the Dubliners. Their seafood is first-rate, but I wouldn't have cared if all they served were breadsticks: you can sit outdoors there, and sitting outdoors in Washington, D.C., in April at twilight is my idea of a good time. Also, I was in a good mood because I couldn't wait to share with Emma, and with Lanny, this latest bit of Washington dissonance—three hundred seventy-five thousand dollars in exchange for a disinterested, good-faith review. Which the taxpayers are already paying me to do anyway.

Windblown Emma was waiting for us at a table by the railing. She had made zero effort to get ready for our date—blue jeans, spads, no makeup—but she had on a cream-colored silk blouse, and wore her sunglasses perched in front of a messy French twist. Those two things were plenty good enough for me. As well as for the waiter and passersby, unfortunately. Lucky I'm not the jealous type.

She kissed both of us full on the lips. Me first, but I thought she might have lingered just a fraction of a second longer on Lanny.

We ordered oysters and drinks. I nearly fell off my wrought-iron chair laughing as I related the tale of the Rockettes and the two sidebar conversations at the fund-raiser. I noticed that Lanny didn't chuckle. This puzzled me.

Momentarily only.

"How come that isn't an *illegal gratuity?*" Emma barked. My head snapped around.

Lanny, no fool, had seen the ref glowering.

"Because that statute applies only to officers of the government," I explained.

"But you're an officer of the government."

"No, I'm not. It's been defined to apply only to the executive branch. Remember I used to make my living indicting people under those laws."

"That doesn't make any sense."

"I didn't say it made sense. I said that's what the courts have held." I took a defensive swig of white wine.

"Well, then, how come it isn't bribery? *That* sure as hell applies to everybody."

"Because it's not in return for me doing something."

"Why do you think they're giving it to you?"

"Doesn't matter. Justice Scalia says you need a quid pro quo. Unanimous Court, not just crazy Nino. It's not a quid pro quo."

"Yes, it is. That's precisely why you think it's funny—and, Lanny, I know damn well you think it's funny, too, so wipe that innocent look off your face—because these people are being so hypocritical."

Hmm. This was food for thought. Why *was* Washington dissonance so funny, anyhow?

"There was no agreement."

"What, you think agreements have to be in writing? You sound like those dumb juries you complain about, that think if you don't have a videotape or a signed confession you can't prove anything. The agreement can be inferred."

I briefly wished Emma had not trained in law. She had opened a cut over my eye with these jabs.

"Lanny says the system makes honest men act like felons," I suggested, looking reproachfully at Lanny.

"No, it makes felons act like felons," said the ref tartly. "Or it makes honest men *into* felons. Al Capone had to start somewhere, sometime."

Lanny swooshed his finger around in his Singapore sling and began singing softly, " 'For he's a jolly good felon, for he's—' "

"Lanny, please!" I had no arguments left, just a naked appeal. It worked, unlike my arguments. There was a moment of silence.

"You're just hot and bothered because you love Martha Holloway because she's a woman," I said to Emma. "Doesn't mean she's always right. The country has gotten along fine with price supports for a long time."

"No, I like Martha Holloway because she's *honest,* unlike just about every other top person in the government. And anybody who could get Phil Vacco appointed U.S. attorney in Boston has pretty good taste, too."

"Okay, I agree with that," I said, hoping to buy more silence.

In fact, I did agree. Phil Vacco was the man I had defeated for Suffolk County district attorney in 1996, a Boston Republican, that rarest of breeds. I had brought him into the DA's office to try white-collar cases and he covered both of us with glory, convicting fifteen banks of currency violations. We tried the cases together. Very high profile, sent me to the U.S. Senate and brought him to the attention of Vice President Hol-

loway. She's a former federal prosecutor, likes straight shoot-
ers, and is in charge of appointing U.S. attorneys for the
Brinker administration.

I thought I might be out of the woods with Emma. I
smiled and tried to exude integrity. It didn't work.

"Let me ask you this." Emma leaned forward on her elbows. "Would you tell the whole conversation to your pal Phil
Vacco, the pillar of rectitude, the prosecutor's prosecutor, if he
was the U.S. attorney down here?"

"You mean, in his professional capacity?"

"No, in case he was a disc jockey. Yes *of course* I mean in
his official capacity, you moron. Oh, sorry!" She thrust her
napkin to her mouth in mock alarm.

I steadied myself. "Well, no. Not because I'd have legal exposure, but because he'd face political exposure, come under
political pressure. To do the wrong thing."

"I think he could handle it." She studied me. Why
wouldn't Lanny throw himself between us?

After a moment, she resumed her attack:

"You know what I think is the wrong thing?"

"I believe so, sweethead, but why don't we hear it anyway."

"I think putting your crown jewels inside a vise operated
by Happy Gilliam is the wrong thing. You said he was standing
right there. Don't get me wrong, I think it's great that he's one-
eighth red-blooded American Indian, I just don't trust him any
further than I can throw him."

Lanny and I looked at each other. This was not just a tren-
chant observation; this was an action-forcing observation.

"Sweetest, I thought you were an idealistic grad student
with your nose in a book, not the latest coming of Metternich.
Anyway, Happy is still planning on running for president of
the United States, he can't afford to be seen double-crossing
people."

"Oh? I would've thought that means he can't afford *not* to
be seen double-crossing people. You think state and city bosses
support candidates for president because they personally love
them?"

"Darling, your newly chosen field, I remind you, is prima-tology. Why not stick to monkeys?"

"I am." She was looking right at me. Why couldn't I have married a chorine?

■

THE NEXT MORNING I SUMMONED Sarah Blakeslee, Rock-ette Supreme and chief lobbyist for all agribusiness interests nationwide, to my suite. She was prompt, dressed like a nun, dark blue suit to the throat. Bustline repressed, too, must be wearing an industrial-strength brassiere.

I don't consider myself paranoid, but I did plan to have a "frank" conversation with her; and anyone who has ever been a federal prosecutor will not have such a conversation in an en-closed space where there might be a microphone recording what is said, no matter how remote the possibility.

"Ms. Blakeslee, so good of you to come, why don't we go for a walk outside."

"That bad, huh? I don't wear wires, you know. Not good for business."

"No, it's just that it's a beautiful day for a walk."

"Except that I forgot my umbrella. I'm not Martha Hol-loway, I won't say you should be investigated by an indepen-dent prosecutor just because you accepted a legal campaign contribution."

This was a first-rate piece of political hit-and-run. Since 1997, the Brinker administration had been stonewalling Dem-ocratic calls for the appointment of an independent prose-cutor to investigate the secretary of commerce, who had apparently prospered in office. There was just one little chink in the stone wall: the vice president of the United States had said that while she had full confidence in Commerce Secretary

Withers, she would have no objection to the appointment of an independent prosecutor, thought it would promote public confidence in the resolution of the matter. Didn't even claim she was misquoted.

The lobbyist community was horrified, and none more so than the lobbyists for agribusiness, who had other reasons to be wary of Ms. Holloway.

"Okay, let's go," I said.

When we had sloshed our way along the magnolia and rhododendrons for a hundred yards or so, and were safely out of range of any mikes, she said in a natural voice: "What's the scoop?"

"Everything's okay on one condition: you give an equal amount, three-seven-five, to Happy Gilliam for his presidential campaign."

"You're not even supporting him, are you?"

Her eyes were worried as she looked up at me, worried she might have missed an item on the who's-sleeping-with-whom whirligig of campaigns in formation and destruction. Washington is never happier than when the major pretenders to the presidency all keep house inside the Beltway. Information is the coin of the realm; proximity makes it easier to come by.

"I mean, not *yet*, that is. Are you?"

"You haven't missed any announcements, if that's what you mean. But . . . you heard me."

First I saw relief, that she hadn't dropped a stitch. Then I saw my message sink in. Then I saw wheels turning as she did some quick calculations and accommodated herself to my message. The bright, confident look returned.

"Senator, we *love* Happy Gilliam. We've raised him much more than that already."

"I know, I mean *on top of*, fresh meat, get me? Or fresh vegetables. And I want him to know it, and I want him to know that I know. But I don't want to talk to him about it."

Sarah Blakeslee looked up and gave me a smile.

"I understand perfectly," she said, and shook my hand. She was the picture of intelligence. "I have to make one stop, but

I'm sure everything will be fine, acceptable. When shall we three meet again?"

We three meet again? Not at all necessary for the game I have in mind. How about bloody not on your life, is that a good start? Didn't she get it?

"That may not be necessary. Let's take it a step at a time."

"Perfect," she said, stopping at the corner of Delaware and shaking my hand again. "Couldn't be better."

A jury would have a tough time finding this lady guilty of anything, I thought as I watched two well-turned ankles retreat briskly up the glistening Avenue.

I LOOKED AROUND. The seagulls were wheeling over Union Station like confetti in an updraft.

That afternoon, Happy Gilliam was on the subway car in front of me in the little tunnel train that takes you from the Capitol back to the Senate office buildings. We were through for the day. I fell in step with him on the platform. He didn't seem surprised.

"Thank you for coming last night, Senator."

"You're more than welcome. You're doing the right thing, they're good people. And I appreciate your initiative this morning."

So Sarah Blakeslee doesn't waste time. But I knew that already.

"Yes, it'll look like we had the biggest party in history together, three hundred seventy-five devoted admirers at two grand a pop."

"No, it won't. They won't be the same channel. And I wouldn't ever mention figures. The walls have ears."

"I appreciate that. I spent seven years in the Justice Department in New York."

"I'm well aware of that."

"But, ah, not to put too fine a point on it, of course, but what is meant by not 'the same channel'? All these federal races are a thousand bucks per person, aren't they?"

"If that's how you take it, they are." He was walking straight ahead, his face virtually tucked into his shirt collar. He might as well have had a hand over his mouth, as Lyndon Johnson used to do. Silly me, I hadn't realized the walls are lined with lip-readers as well as ears.

"And if that's how you take it," he muttered, "you're a fool."

This could have meant a number of things. There's hard money, there's soft money. There are formal campaign committees, and there are political action committees. And independent expenditures. And educational nonprofits. I didn't say anything, just kept walking.

"Take it in your official campaign committee," said Happy, "all you guarantee is the get-a-life libs at Common Cause are going to scream at you for every dime."

"So, the source of my thr—, my amount, and, uh, the other amount, might not be the same?"

"Source will be absolutely the same." He stopped at his office door, shook my hand, smiled for the camera that was not there. "Enough said," he whispered. "Maybe too much said, in fact." He clapped me on the shoulder and said in a normal voice, "Just a word to the wise." He pushed open the massive door, revealing a beehive and a wedgie, both over bursting polka-dot dresses.

"I get it," I said. Then I wished I hadn't.

Happy had already turned. Had he heard me? The door closed slowly, heavily, behind him. Everything about Happy Gilliam was heavy.

A word to the wise.

I didn't feel wise. There is a word, though, a legal word, for what I felt like.

I felt like a coconspirator.

■

EVENTS LEFT ME NO TIME to regroup. Both Washington dailies led their Saturday editions the next morning with a richly detailed account of financial and ethical transgressions on the part of Simon Buffington, the deputy attorney general of the United States. Both papers cited official sources. Neither paper had called Buffington for comment. No other newspaper in the country had the story.

This was a classic inside-the-Beltway bag job. Whoever had leaked these facts was powerful enough to insist that the story run as dictated, without being balanced by any outraged reaction from the subject or his allies. Newspapers don't like to do that, so the source had to be someone they would need to depend on in the future, or they wouldn't have gone along with the deal.

By midmorning, Buffington and his boss, Harry Frobisch, were firing back, stressing the usual two completely inconsistent points: number one, this is all hogwash and completely false; number two, this is an outrageous and highly illegal leak of confidential grand jury information, a criminal investigation of the leak has already been undertaken, whoever gave this scurrilous material to the papers is in big trouble, in fact anyone who doesn't shut up about this may be violating grand jury secrecy, etc.

I had seen this defensive gambit executed many times before, but never more smoothly or forcefully than by Simon Buffington. He spoke for thirty minutes without notes at his press conference, seamlessly rebutting each factual allegation and simultaneously lambasting the faceless and sinister forces behind all this lawless innuendo. Buffington had stood number one in his class at Harvard Law School thirty years earlier. He now wore rimless round spectacles, tinted brown. It was impossible not to think of Trotsky.

By midafternoon, every Democratic officeholder in Washington was on TV clamoring for the appointment of an independent prosecutor. Except me. I didn't think I had enough facts, I told the press. I didn't add that I was so sick of seeing senators on television pompously reading from pieces of paper that said, "Let no one be a judge in his own cause!" and "Who shall guard the guards themselves?" that I wanted to throw up in my briefcase.

I also didn't add that I was feeling a little tender about allegations of financial impropriety these days.

■

TWO DAYS LATER was the annual White House reception for freshman members of Congress.

Washington's oddest couple, Myron Brinker and Martha Holloway, stood in a receiving line just inside the East Room. Brinker's people made sure three protocol officers as well as Hortense Brinker stood between them, well spaced out. The *Tribune* had to use a wide-angle lens to get the two of them into the same shot for the next day's edition, capturing the contrast between her peroxide blond exuberance and his coffinlike air.

Wonders of modern technology, I thought, when I saw the photo. In Trotsky's day, they would have airbrushed out the people between them.

And then airbrushed Trotsky, too, come to think of it. Maybe we *are* making progress. . . .

This mandatory Washington occasion was—how shall we say it?—a delicate one. Most of the freshmen were Democrats. Brinker hated them and they hated him. All anyone could think about was Simon Buffington, and no one could mention his name. In the president's house, it would have been too impolite. It was like ignoring a mastodon in the receiving line. We all asked each other, "What's new with you?" and received prompt replies: "Oh nothing much, what's new with you? Anything? Or nothing?" "Not much. Nothing, really."

Martha Holloway wore a gray pinch-waist jacket and skirt with navy trim, cut to two inches above the knee. She was about five foot nine but wore heels, and her obviously dyed bouffant hairdo made her taller than Myron Brinker. A single strand of pearls at the neck, both wrists covered with bracelets. No rings: she had never married and perhaps wanted no mistaking that. She was forty-seven and looked five years younger.

Her welcome of me and Emma was more electrical than physical.

"Senator, Mrs. Mullally, so *good* of you to come!," sweeping us along with arm and words. "I followed and *admired* your career in law enforcement, Senator, both in New York and especially Boston, you broke new ground there with the bank cases, and of course we're *thrilled* you produced Phil Vacco for us, he's simply one of our star U.S. attorneys, I consult him *constantly* about field issues in the Justice Department, isn't it *awful* about Simon Buffington, they should just have independent investigations and clear the air with both him and Secretary Bob Withers, don't you think, Mr. *Congressman!* So good to see you thanks so *much* for . . ."

At this point, I could no longer hear her voice and realized we were a good ten feet downstream, abreast of an obviously unhappy protocol officer who had not enjoyed the veep's remark about Buffington and the commerce secretary. I was studying his face with amusement when he opened his mouth and said, "Mr. President, Senator Mullally."

I looked down into unsmiling little red pig eyes.

"Honored to meet you, Mr. President," I said.

"Mullally, yes, you are the tall one, aren't you? Well, you beat a great man in Harold Dellenbach. Harold was one of our lions."

"Thank you for having us, sir," said Emma, taking his hand. "Mr. President."

"Yes," he said.

What a pill. I wasn't thinking about him, however, as we waited for our car at the west vehicle entrance.

I followed your career in law enforcement in New York. What the hell was that supposed to mean? I was a medium-level assistant U.S. attorney in Brooklyn, she was governor of Florida. She never would have followed my career there.

She must have *gone back* and followed it. Later. After I got elected a senator. Maybe even after she talked with her fair-haired boy Phil Vacco, my best friend in law enforcement.

My best friend on top of the table, anyway.

■

THAT NIGHT I DREAMED of Detective Lieutenant Rudy Solano, my deer-hunting buddy, my fellow crime-fighter, who got me my job as an assistant U.S. attorney in Brooklyn. My dead buddy.

At first, he was a benign figure in my dream, giving me a sense of belonging, washing away the terrible sense of poverty and social isolation I had felt at the orphanage and the foster home.

Then I saw the money on the bed, I saw the cheap metal bedpost, the bare lightbulb. My one-room apartment. Three years I lived there. Dreams don't have time to be subtle. That was the first time I took too much money, money that didn't belong to me. Thanks, Rudy.

Then, still in his police uniform, Rudy Solano was a judge, pointing at me, lecturing me: How could *you* do this? I was a prisoner in the dock, I was on trial. I looked over at the witness box. Sarah Blakeslee and her fellow lobbyists were dancing there, in full stage dress. U.S. and foreign currency was spilling from their décolletés. They seemed unaware of my presence.

Judge/Lieutenant Solano directed me not to look at them. I felt ashamed. I looked anyway. The top of the junior Rockette's dress finally gave up the fight and fell off. No supports there, industrial or otherwise: full breasts, straight out, bright aureoles, staring right at me. No, wait, they were eyes, scornful eyes. They were Solano's eyes.

Solano's face began to sweat and shake, as I had seen it do in life. He fell from the judge's bench, landing in the snow, in hunting clothes covered with blood, as I had found him when Sergeant Gatto drove me up to Jaffrey that Saturday night. I was there, in the snow, in my dream. The yellow tape from the police barrier stuck to my clothes. It was still there the next day when I walked into my office in the Hart Senate Office Building. Everyone was staring at it. How am I going to explain this snow, this tape?

Emma was dabbing at my temples and forehead with a cool washcloth.

"What? What's that? What are you doing? What time is it?"

"Nothing, honeybun, nothing, you were just giving a speech, is all."

"About what?"

"You said, 'Rudy, stop it, that's enough, you're not hanging me out to dry. Gilliam's in too.' "

I stared at her.

"We don't by any chance feel guilty about what we did with Happy Gilliam, do we? Or Rudy Solano, maybe?"

Had I muttered something about Rudy falling, bleeding? That must be erased. Of course, I never saw that happen. Must shield Emma, save myself.

"What else did I say?"

"That's all, my poor baby. I just hate to see you sweat like this. You must have a fever." She kissed my temple. I felt a vein pulsing against her lips. Hope she didn't notice. Wait, why? It was only a bad dream!

"Well, there's obviously no connection, just dream logic. The stuff with Gilliam may not be the *Daily Mail*'s cup of tea, but it's completely legal under current law. Not that an independent prosecutor couldn't change the rules on you at any time."

Emma patted my arm.

"Yes, dear, it's very worrisome that they could change the rules and not give you a written opinion in advance as to what's illegal. Now go back to sleep."

I didn't want this sarcastic line pursued any further, so I rolled onto my side and closed my eyes, even though my mind was racing and I now wasn't sleepy at all. I had been giving too many hostages to fortune.

Part Two

I DON'T MEAN TO TELL YOU that all my problems in Washington were caused by others. Well before Happy Gilliam got me overextended with the agribusiness crowd in April, I had stepped in it pretty good all by myself. This was in January, right after Emma and I hit town.

Here's the deal: I get there, national press is loving me, six foot four, black hair, lantern jaw, good on his feet, state adjoins first-in-the-nation New Hampshire primary—I'm thinking I have the situation pretty well covered, okay? And this view is shared by Lanny Green, who had been my campaign manager. Lanny comes by his political instincts honestly, cut his baby teeth organizing food service workers for the AFL-CIO. So we feel, well, undefeated. And we are.

All we have to do is decide whom to support for majority leader of the Senate. Simple enough.

Lanny swings by our modest house in the southeast corner of Georgetown at ten on January 17, a Sunday morning, to review the bidding. You can sail a Frisbee into Rock Creek from the back porch, right between two dead gingkos. The front yard is dominated by a eucalyptus tree. That tree is why I bought the place: it's a constant and pleasing reminder that I've moved well south of Brighton, Massachusetts, and South Brooklyn, New York, my two hometowns.

The fruit of the eucalyptus has a little *Y* in it, like the old New York City subway tokens. I pick one up and put it in my change pocket on the way out the door every morning. There's no turnstile in my reserved parking space by the Hart Building, so I keep the eucalyptus nut in my pocket all day and toss it into my yard just before I open the picket fence gate at night. Emma is generally waiting for me on the stoop, reading a book, big smile on her face, hair piled carelessly on top of her gorgeous head, showing off her long neck. But I digress.

There is a bay window in our living room. Lanny and I are sitting on opposite sides. Emma, carrying three dog-eared issues of *Science News,* parks herself on the floor yoga-style in front of the fireplace and lights her cigarette from the bottom of the flame. "Mind if I sit in?"

"Honey, this is *serious,*" I whine. "We're meeting Happy Gilliam at the Pied de Mouton at eleven-thirty and we have to know what to *do.*"

Emma laughs in my face, takes a drag, and blows the smoke in my eyes for good measure.

"Ohh, I seeee," she concludes. "The future of the universe." She takes a puff. "Equals boy talk. Sure. Stands to reason." She takes another drag and I move out of range.

"Maybe you boyos should read this, to guide your deliberations." She tosses a *Science News* at my feet.

"What's this, sweetie?"

"It's the coming-out party of the bonobos. They're our closest ape relative—a kind of first cousin of the chimpanzees, people didn't even know they were different until well into this century. Female-dominated society. Don't spend as much time as the chimps jockeying for position about who's going to be the alpha male—that's Greek for the dominant male, Lan, I know you went to the school of hard knocks—so they have more time to sit around and eat and, ah, do other things."

"They're not sexually promiscuous, by any chance?" I venture.

"They're completely promiscuous." Emma slinks over and puts her tongue in my ear. "They're very smart."

"Lose the bonobos," says Lanny. "We don't work in the girls' clubhouse, we work in the chimpanzees' clubhouse, and we're going to play by chimp rules." He turns to Emma. "There are fifty-two votes in the caucus. Your candidates for leader, both of whom are also interested in Myron Brinker's lodgings at 1600 Pennsylvania, are Happy Gilliam from the Panhandle, honest Injun and kind of a cross between James Eastland of Mississippi and Lister Hill of Alabama; and Anson Vivian, southern highlander and the pride of Big Ugly, West Virginia, a perfect cross between Fred Harris of Oklahoma and Harold Hughes of Iowa."

"Those guys all senators?" asks Emma.

"Yeh, I figured I'd keep it simple," says Lanny grudgingly.

"Could you do that with governors too?"

"Yeh, you wanna hear? Gilliam would be a cross—"

"Lanny, *stop!*" I shout. "Let's *go!*" I wave my arms as though doing the butterfly backwards.

"Okay. Newspapers say, and pundit consensus is, Gilliam has leader wrapped up, about thirty committed votes for that, even though of course he's too conservative to win any primary north of Mason-Dixon for POTUS."

"POTUS?" Emma's eyebrows shoot up.

"President of the United States. Secret Servicespeak."

"How many uncommitted?"

"Nobody knows for sure, but you're looking at one of them," says Lanny. "Actually, you're not, but he's right over there." Lanny is trying to get Emma to take her stare somewhere else, anywhere else.

Emma could have been either a great hunter or a great wild animal. She will wait all day and then charge her target four times in a minute. "What do you mean, Gilliam has *about* thirty votes?" she asks. "How many is it? We're only talking about fifty-two Democrats, that's a single deck of cards, no jokers, I know you can count cards, Lan."

"Counting votes in the Senate when it's a secret ballot is like herding squirrels, sweetheart. In fairness to Lanny, there are forty jokers in that pack."

"Won't they tell you?"

I tick off the responses, the obvious responses, on my fingers. "Number one, they might tell you and change their mind. Number two, we think we know already, having assessed the situation and their possible motivations. We did that with some success in Massachusetts, remember. Number three, the old Uncertainty Principle. If you ask them point-blank, you may roil the equilibrium. Don't want to disturb that meniscus. Plus, four, if you ask them, it proves you don't know, which makes you look stupid. Also, five, in looking for an answer, you're forcing them to do something they don't want to do."

"You guys really *are* chimps. All chivvying. Chivvying and display." Emma has enrolled in the Ph.D. program in anthropology at Johns Hopkins; it seems she is having a hard time giving animal behavior a rest.

Now she is off onto other game.

"What are you going to ask for, over and above your pig's knuckles and veal shank?"

Lanny purses his lips. "I'm not entirely sure we should ask for anything."

"I agree," I say. "We're going to have to live with this guy for a long time. We're going to have to depend on him for a long time. No sense setting his teeth on edge. Over the long run, it's better to get off on the right foot by showing him that we trust him."

"But why should you trust him?"

"I didn't say we *do* trust him, I said that we should *show* him that we trust him."

"Oh, I see. You mean, lie."

"Not a lie at all. Only statements are lies. Show him that we trust him. Besides, trust is ambiguous. Anyway, you said that, not me. Also it never happened, and if it did, it was a long time ago."

Emma laughs and blows out smoke. "Wow. So that's your story and you're sticking with it?"

I nod. "Trust me on this. I'm pretty sure." I smile amiably, to show I am understating, underselling. Always undersell, Lanny and I tell the staff. What goes around comes around.

Of course, I am far from sure, but I can't let anyone see that, not even Emma or Lanny. It's a seven-day-a-week poker game in my line of work—with constituents, with other pols, most of all with the media. If people get the feeling you don't have confidence in your own hand, they'll never let you bluff, somebody will chase you and call you every time, you'll never run up those big margins that come with a successful bluff. So you internalize: never let them see you sweat, don't look back because something might be gaining on you, play 'em like you got 'em. At this point, I don't know how my vote for majority leader is going to go, but I trust myself to base it on the right combination of research and hunch.

■

THOUGH THE PREVIOUS two days' weather has been arctic by Washington standards, the Sunday-morning sun is strong. There is melting ice on every sidewalk in Georgetown, steam issuing from the folds of bark in the maple and locust trees. These conditions give my heart a lift as we pick our way west on P Street. I love the incongruities that a change in weather produces.

I suspect the P Street route has been selected by my still upwardly mobile bride to facilitate an inspection of the snow-laden rhodies, azaleas, and mountain laurel. Plantings scream as loud as hard currency in Georgetown, you might as well look right into the abutter's cash drawer, same voyeuristic pleasure.

Emma kicks at a brick wall until she dislodges a large sheet of ice. Still she is not content. She halts.

"Are you sure you're not overanalyzing?" she asks.

"Honey, we're not analyzing at all. This is an art, not a science. Maybe we're gliding by the seat of our pants, but that's what the great ones do. Politics ain't driving a car, it's driving a boat. At best."

Emma can see we are dug in.

"Let's swoop down Wisconsin like Mosby's Raiders!" she cries in a new voice.

"How do you know about Mosby?" asks Lanny suspiciously. He is a fanatical admirer of the Confederate forces.

"I don't. I just like him. And Jackson, of course. And Jubal Early and Nathan Bedford Forrest, even if he did go a little weird after the war." Lanny takes a courtly bow in her direction. She bows back.

"You look gray around the gills, at least, Lan."

"Obliged, ma'am." He doffs an imaginary Confederate cap.

After swooping down Wisconsin, we duck into the Pied de Mouton, where we meet a haze of Gauloise and Gitane smoke at eye level. Lanny and Emma tip their heads back and inhale gratefully.

There are four tight-sweatered chicks—sorry, there's no other word—at the corner bench by the window.

"We have your table ready out back, Mr. Green." Lanny is a regular.

"We'll wait for that one." Lanny indicates a mess of used plates adjacent to the lucky bench.

Emma takes his elbow and guides us to the bar. She leans close to Lanny, inclining her head.

"Lanny, for heaven's sake. Why do you be so transparent about sitting next to those poor girls?"

Emma means two things by this. First, the consensus on the Hill and in Boston is that Lanny is gay, since no one has ever seen him with a female date. But since he works all the time, we're not sure, and we're certainly not asking. Second, if Lanny is not gay, Emma would dearly love to marry him off to Jerry Traugott, my gum-chewing, street-talking press secretary. So Emma is scouting.

"Objects of beauty, my dear. I like the way they hold themselves, hold their cigarettes, for that matter. They care about themselves. Just 'cause I don't want to bed 'em, doesn't mean I can't admire 'em. Jerry T. and I are crazy about each other, for example, but we don't exactly want to settle down and have kids."

"Well, I think actually she does"—Lanny looks quickly at

Emma—"but I take your point, I take your point entirely," she concludes tactfully.

Lanny sticks out his chin at Emma in a mock hit-me attitude. "Most natural thing in the world," he says. "You shouldn't have any question about it." The moment of danger has passed; they are back into mutual joshing.

Lanny wordlessly scores two Gitanes from a stranger at the bar and gives one to Emma. She holds his wrist as he lights hers. Just like Lauren Bacall. If that doesn't make you heterosexual, Lan, nothing's going to.

Not to intrude, I study the bottles above the bar. Individually, they are unremarkable, but collectively they are beautiful, especially if you let your eye sweep them. Square to soft-shouldered, tapering to ramrod-straight, green, brown, silver and gold, glittering and dull—they are a canvas. Hopper? No, too much detail. I must study art, I know nothing about painting. I squint to frame my canvas. I want to eat those bottles, not drink them. They remind me of the miniature groceries in a see-through sack that Sister Francine gave me for Christmas one year at the orphanage. I loved those cans of Campbell's soup, those carrots in abandon. I never thanked her adequately, never really thanked her at all. One of the abiding regrets of my life. Still wakes me up at night, and during daydreams. Must go back and thank Sister Francine.

I become aware the bartender is staring at me, so I lift my eyes casually. I study a blackboard nestled twixt bourbon and rum. Its frame bears the legend "Saranac, the spirit of the Adirondacks." The fruit of a farewell party is captured in chalk, in a firm hand: "You ALL lie—You ALL hide. No . . . you're not like ME! I ALWAYS tell the truth—even when I lie! So say good night to the BAD GIRL! Because this is the LAST time you will ever see THIS BAD GIRL AGAIN!"

Lanny sees me reading. "That was Esmeralda," he says. "She was a piece of work. Went back to Brazil. Broke everybody's heart here. Left that for us in the back room."

"For anyone in particular?" asks Emma.

"No, just for, you know, the, uh, group."

"I see," says Emma, tapping her ash triumphantly. Lanny ordinarily plays a good game of cards, but his face now is a book. A children's book.

He looks away from Emma. She is a tough crowd, all by herself.

Lanny rallies: "Pepper, a Yurchenko shooter for the lady."

"Oh no, my no," cries Emma, staring at the bottles and splaying her fingers against her chin in mimicry of thought. This lady could do stand-up. "I believe I'll start with a teeny-weeny Tullamore Dew, or perhaps a bit of Lochnagar Royal or, say, do you have any Glenmorangie?" Pepper, agape, tries to move in several directions at once and becomes immobilized.

■

At this delicate moment, Senator Harlan Gilliam of Texas, ducking his head, pushes through the door with three aides, frowning furiously about something. The aides are whispering. Gilliam catches sight of us, dips one temple to an aide to indicate they are to disappear, and breaks into a beaming smile, two rows, all in a split second.

"Senator!" he pronounces with tremendous charm and admiration. "I am so *glad* to *see* you! And is this *Mrs.* Mullally?" He takes Emma's defenseless hand in both of his. "And—" He turns to Lanny but evidently cannot think who Lanny might be. Nonetheless, he holds his expression of joyful anticipation.

I put him out of his misery quick. "Yes, this is Emma, and this is Lanny Green, my AA."

"Mr. Green, I've heard so *much* about you! You all ran such a brilliant race against Harold, I mean Senator Dellenbach, *former* Senator Dellenbach, and we are so *pleased* to have you!" Emma finds something interesting on the ceiling.

Pepper sees us to our table.

The would-be leader of the free world looks his part as well as he plays it. He is an enormous man, six foot five and easily 250 pounds, well distributed. His Harris coat and creased twill trousers seem to have fallen on him from a great height. He wears an open red flannel shirt, two buttons undone—my style all the way—with quite a good deal of chest hair visible, mixed red and white. He obviously doesn't care what anybody thinks about this.

His dark skin passes for an outdoorsman's tan. He has a fine aquiline nose, cheeks and chin strong, eyes gray, bushy black brows in a class with Holmes and Learned Hand. His full head of dark red hair, which the gray has not yet reached, is brushed straight back and stays there. The effect of the whole is to convey size and power equally.

Gilliam flashes another crocodile smile as we sit down, and places his paw solicitously on my wrist. I see something flit across his eyes: surprise not to find a Rolex there, perhaps.

"I know this is going to be a difficult decision for you, Senator," he begins. "Of course, you know I'd like to be the Leader, but we're really not here to discuss me or my prospects. What I would like is to get a better sense of *your* preferences, for the course you would like to chart in the Senate. Have you given any thought to committee assignments, for example?"

Funny he should mention that. I have to give him credit: he goes straight for the hoop, no dribbling around.

"Why, Senator, you are most kind, and of course I have, at least a little. Finance would be a . . . well, a plum—and perhaps not inapposite, given my background with money laundering and white collar criminal cases. When I was a prosecutor—"

He cuts me right off. "Of course, of course, I know about that, Senator, and I think that makes all the sense in the world. What further?"

I can feel myself unwinding, basking. When the waiter brings our cassoulets, I do not even fall to my food like a madman. This is uncharacteristic. Emma says after 11:00 A.M. I am like a dog, the only more dangerous place in Washington than between a candidate and a TV camera is between me and my meal.

"Beyond that, Senator, of course being on the coast in the Northeast so close to Europe, I have always had an interest in foreign relations, at least I have recently . . ." I am fumbling. I hurry on. "But, of course, that would be entirely up to yourself. I don't really think I have any surprising preferences. Appropriations, Budget, would be wonderful. Agriculture I don't have much of a constituency, beyond cranberries. But anything would be fine, except Judiciary."

"Your thinking?"

"Abortion, immigration—and I've got a big foreign-born population—boring judges nominated by Myron Brinker and Harry Frobisch in their own image—" Gilliam's smile freezes. "Of course, I hold no brief against the president," I add hurriedly, "I simply think his judges are, well, by and large not that interesting."

I am waiting for the expression to lighten up. It doesn't. I have struck a sour note somewhere. Maybe Attorney General Harry Frobisch's image is Gilliam's image, too. Different parties, but both big crude men who have been doing exactly as they please for a long time. Yes, that's probably it.

Gilliam clears his throat. "You have sized it up remarkably, Senator, not that that surprises me, given all I have heard of you. Judiciary is nothing but two miles of bad road, as we say in my state."

He pulls a sheet of paper from his breast pocket.

"Not to be overdirect, Senator"—he has not looked at Emma or Lanny, I am the only person in the room—"but this is a, ah, list, well not really a list so much as an, ah, informed assessment, of some of those whom I have reason to believe are favorably disposed toward my candidacy. For the Leader's position, that is," he adds sharply.

There are twenty-six names on the list. This is four fewer than the total accorded to Gilliam by the media, as he must surely know. I take this detail as an indication of the strength of commitment of the twenty-six.

Lanny evidently has read the list upside down. "You have Wonham from Kentucky? I thought he was leaning Vivian."

"Senator Wonham and, ah, a number of the Border State senators have been troubled by the stance of the distinguished gentleman from West Virginia, on, ah, certain, ah, *agricultural* issues," Gilliam explains, and turns to beam his brightest lamps at every person at the table, including Emma for the first time. She flashes back at him like a champion.

Gilliam returns to me. Again, there is no one else in the room. "Senator, it will not have escaped your notice that twenty-six is one-half of fifty-two, and that your vote will, would, put me over the top. Your sure vote. I am not interested in talking in generalities. Well, I guess I never am, and least of all now!" He laughs heartily, and claps Lanny on the shoulder. Lanny, taken by surprise, forces an out-loud laugh that is part cough and part bark. Not a success. Gilliam falls back to business.

"It would, will, mean an awful lot to me. It would . . . well, it would open a lot of doors."

"Doors that say 'Finance' and 'Foreign Relations' on them?" The question is from Lanny.

Mistake, breaking conversational rhythm. Must find moment to talk with Lanny tactfully about the uses of silence. Wait 'til someone else makes same mistake in his presence. That will be right moment. Draw Lanny aside, complain about other person. Carom shot more tactful, more effective. Wait, here I am with Gilliam. I want something. What is it? Mustn't daydream.

Gilliam smiles broadly. "In the fullness of time, I am more than confident that all that laundry will sort itself out."

He sees immediately this is not enough for me. "Finance I would consider a definite," he avers. My fork drops like an osprey to spear a veal shank, signaling this is a plus. Gilliam stabs a sausage, grinning at me the while, to show he is in on the game. Emma studies the ceiling some more. Gilliam passes me a slip of paper with a telephone number on it.

"This rings on my desk," he says.

Play 'em like you got 'em. He plainly has 'em.

■

WE WALK BACK ALONG R STREET. "Time to consult the trees," says Emma. Her view is that at moments of decision, trees are a more helpful guide than warm bird entrails. I am in her camp on this. It amazes us that Edgar Allan Poe stands alone in literature as a priest of vegetable sentience. We both think the whole premise of the animal-vegetable-mineral divide is ludicrously anthropocentric. Emma says plant biology is racist because it's directed at using plants to feed, clothe, and house a burgeoning, unnecessary funguslike population: namely, humans.

Emma reads aloud to Lanny from the plaque at the corner of Dumbarton Oaks: "Trees are noble elements to be protected by successive generations and are not to be neglected or lightly destroyed."

"Okay by me," says Lanny. He obviously couldn't care less.

A dozen crows are going crazy at the edge of Montrose Park. Probably have an owl cornered, maybe a snowy. We walk through the park and Oak Hill cemetery, looking for signs. On the shiniest, smallest headstone of all, someone has placed a fresh rose, a rose that still has droplets of water on it. I move it with my foot to read the inscription: "Sarah Hill, died December 18, 1998, aged 22 years, beloved wife of William Hill." I put that rose back fast and do not look up as we are exiting the cemetery. I am not interested in signs anymore. There is no question in my mind that to look up would be to look into the eyes, the distraught eyes, the furious eyes, of William Hill, aged approximately twenty-two years and very recently widowed.

THE APPOINTMENT WITH ANSON VIVIAN is for four o'clock that afternoon at our house. The overtones from the chime of our grandfather clock are still echoing when he knocks. The day has grown bitterly cold; his breath hangs heavy as I open the door. He is unescorted, and coatless. He gratefully accepts a mug of tea, for warmth, I daresay, and we settle again in the living room.

Vivian is speaking, but I am not listening. I am forming impressions, in a hurry. On the plus side, he seems genuinely friendly, not just courtly. His carriage conveys energy. He is under six feet, has the lope of an athlete, a wiry build, black hair streaked with white. There is perhaps something of Napoleon Bonaparte about him, something of Shimon Peres, the great Israeli leader. But dreams aren't votes, Anson, I find myself musing.

On the downside, he seems half Gilliam's size, half his presence. Both men are in their late forties, but Vivian seems older. He acts hesitant, almost nervous.

After the first fifteen seconds, it doesn't matter what Vivian says. I won't believe him if he produces a sheaf of thirty-five written pledges.

As it happens, he doesn't have a list with him at all. Explains he doesn't want to tip off Gilliam, who is counting some Vivian people in his column. Lanny and I exchange a glance at *that* one.

Vivian's mouth is still working when I say, "I understand," and stand up. I have heard enough. He seems startled, and stands up as well. I say, "Well, Senator, thank you very much for coming by, especially on such a nippy day. Let us take all this under advisement, and one of us will be back with you before the vote on Tuesday."

Vivian shoots me a look. He knows that taking a matter "under advisement" is as close as an experienced politician gets to saying "not on your life." Also the "one of us" is even more brutal than I intend. Nonetheless, he manfully returns his mug to the sink, drops a used teabag in the wastebasket, admires our kitchen tiles, bids us a pleasant good afternoon, and marches out into the cold, his hands in his pockets. From the bay, Lanny and I follow his progress as far as the corner. He looks small, isolated.

Emma curls up again by the fire as we are conducting our postmortem.

"What's your take?"

"He's already given away all his choice committee assignments, and I personally would be doubtful he's got the fourteen votes the papers are giving him," Lanny summarizes.

"I agree," I add. "And he doesn't have a list, or he left it at home, or the dog ate it, or it blew off the porch, and Gilliam does have a list, and it's four less than the papers are giving him, which means it's probably rock solid. It's all over but the shouting. Gilliam will have the entire South, three from the Farm Belt because they owe him bigtime from the last tax bill and some price support stuff, plus there's several fire-breathers from New England and the Rockies who staked their careers on the immigration bill and he delivered for them. In addition, we're picking up that he may have made a deal with a few folks from power-producing states, Ohio, Pennsylvania, Indiana, about limits on sulfur dioxide emissions, basically agreeing to soften some sections of the Clean Air Act."

"But, Terry, you hate that! That's just the sort of thing you campaigned against! That's why you're here!"

"Sweetheart, Lanny and I are not saying we *like* Happy Gilliam. We don't particularly like Happy Gilliam. What we're saying is that Happy Gilliam has the *votes*. At a time like this, you're sure as hell better off being with the winner than with the loser."

"Well, but for what? I don't see why you can't go with who you like."

"We don't like anybody," says Lanny. "Or dislike. This isn't personal, this is business." He turns to me. "Boss, to be on the safe side, I think I should double-check tomorrow with the AAs for Sagebrush Sam and Mr. Peanut, and nose around a little bit about that group of four from Pollution, Incorporated. If that deal's real, Gilliam's going to go over thirty whether anybody likes it or not."

"Sounds good."

Emma sighs. Lanny leaves, shaking his head. Obvious. Everything is obvious.

■ ■ ■

ON MONDAY, Lanny reports back to me at 4:30 P.M.

"Mr. Peanut and Sagebrush Sam are with Gilliam all the way, as we figured. The other guys, Pollution, Inc., aren't talking to their staffs, say they like everybody, but staff's best take is at worst an even split."

"That will put Gilliam over the top," I observe.

"Yep." Lanny is smiling. "Boss, no time like the present for you to make that call."

I punch in the number that rings on Gilliam's desk. It is answered on the second ring.

"Happy Gilliam."

"Senator, this is Terry Mullally calling. I—"

"Yes, Senator. Thank you so much for calling! I, I . . ." His voice is a strained whisper.

"Well, not at all. I just want to let you know that I will be with you all the way in the morning."

"Oh, why that's swell, that's just swell, I'm sure you'll never regret it—"

"And if there's anything else I can do—"

"No, that's, that's, you're very kind. Good-bye, Senator."

"Good-bye, Leader!"

I look at the receiver for a moment. "That was strange."

"What?"

"I think he'd already hung up when I called him 'Leader.' Sort of a funny time to break off a conversation like that. And he was whispering. Why is he whispering in his own office?"

"He probably has three groups who hate each other hovering around, trying to get on board the train."

This has only to be heard to be believed. I thank my stars for Lanny.

■

THE NEXT MORNING, TUESDAY, the nineteenth of January, there is a gauntlet of forty or fifty TV cameras as the members of the world's most exclusive club stride into the Democratic caucus room in the Capitol. As usual, the members seem drawn to their full height and then some by the klieg lights. On this occasion, it is more important to be seen striding purposefully into the caucus room than it is to tarry and banter, so stride purposefully we do. The lead Hill correspondent for the *Washington Tribune* shouts at Vivian as he hurries in, "Senator! Can you tell us your reaction to the news of a final surge to Senator Gilliam? Are you disappointed?"

Vivian smiles gamely and waves her off. He points into the caucus room and disappears inside. I feel sorry for him. No one likes taking a pasting in public, but that's show biz.

There is no chitchat as we settle into our felt-lined seats at the two long tables set up for the occasion. The nominations of Gilliam and Vivian are made and seconded in less than a minute. I make no attempt to conceal my ballot from my neighbors as I mark it "Gilliam" and hand it to the waiting aide from the secretary's office. Most of the other members are careful to shield their ballots with their hands, and fold them twice. I lean back in my chair and fold my arms.

In three or four minutes, the secretary of the Senate, the affable and popular Hobie Furlong of Louisiana, rises to announce the results. I give him my rapt attention.

"Mr. Gilliam of Texas, twenty-four votes."

My feet drop to the floor. I lean forward in my chair, putting my elbows on the table. I feel my face flush. I look around to see if anyone else is concerned the secretary may have misspoken. There is a wall of blank faces.

A lot of people must have not voted. I didn't think that was the practice on this sort of vote. I see Anson Vivian looking straight at me. I have not called him back since the weekend.

The secretary pauses. Why is he pausing? Finally, he clears his throat to begin again. Not a moment too soon. I am running low on oxygen.

"Mr. Vivian of West Virginia, Mr. Vivian of West Virginia . . ."

Yes, you fool, we know his name and where he's from, tell us how many *votes* he has, and why so many of Gilliam's people abstained. Go on, tell us, you idiot!

"Mr. Vivian of West Virginia, twenty-eight votes."

A roar of approval goes up around the room. Happy Gilliam is the first to reach the new majority leader and congratulate him.

Vivian gives me a warm smile as I finally get to the head of the line to shake his hand. "Terry, I appreciate your consideration, and I understand entirely," he says under his breath so that only I can hear. I feel somewhat less horror-struck than I was a moment before. This is a presence. This is power. Wait. He called me by my first name: is that good or bad? Wait.

No one waits. Outside the caucus room, there is a quick show of Democratic unity and a punchy pep talk by majority leader Vivian, in which he sketches his plans for the session. I am in the crush of senators just in front of him, looking up into his face for clues. He smilingly demurs when asked whether his leadership team has a place for Senator Gilliam. New committee assignments, he says, will be handled that afternoon, so the members can begin work immediately on the many weighty issues within their responsibilities.

As the majority leader concludes his remarks and waves off the mikes, I hear a sibilant voice in my ear: "Next time fold your ballot, kid."

I wheel around. No one's in sight, or, rather, everyone's in sight. There are half a dozen senators within three feet of me. All stone faces. I start to scan their expressions, but the crowd surges and I am carried off to the side. I peer back into the crowd, but there's no telling who might have hissed those words.

If anyone did.

I walk back to the office in a daze. Each succeeding hall-way seems more interminable than the last. When I see my name, I fumble with the doorknob, and fleetingly wonder if the locks on my office have been changed. Then I remember I am still a United States senator, and put on my confident expression as I walk in.

The receptionist looks, well, there is no other way to say it: the receptionist looks as though the dog died. Lanny is standing by the water cooler, holding a piece of paper, pale as death. We look at each other.

"Come on in," I say finally.

No one says anything to us as we walk back to my inner office. Lanny closes the door. I sit behind my desk, put my palms on the blotter, and blow out a lungful of air.

"Funny town," I say.

"It gets worse," says Lanny.

"How?"

"Committee assignments." He hands me the sheet of paper.

I read: Judiciary, Agriculture, Ethics.

I reread it: no change.

"It doesn't get any worse than this, does it?"

"No, Boss, it doesn't. It can't. And Vivian has settled Happy Gilliam's hash nicely. Harlan is the proud new chairman of Agriculture, which as you know he despises, he'd much rather hang out with the silk stocking crowd, all those Panhandlers are Houston wannabes. Plus, ninety percent of the country thinks the Ag Committee and the tobacco lobby are the same thing, so he's carrying a forty-pound deadweight to 2000."

The door swings open. No reason it should startle me, but it does. It is Jerry Traugott, the press secretary. Snappy new white and gold dress, seems all wrong for the moment, but probably just as well not to be in full mourning.

"Sorry, fellas, life goes on. Marian Stultz from the *Tribune* wants to know how you voted, are you happy with committee assignments, etc."

Lanny seems to regroup a little at this, grateful to have something to occupy his mind, other than how stupid we are.

"Tell her secret ballot, but we couldn't be more pleased with the committees, Ethics a personal priority of the senator's since his corruption-fighting days in the DA's office, Agriculture very important to the cranberry crop of Massachusetts, of course, and Judiciary—"

"I know, I know. For us, Judiciary is the best committee in the entire United States Senate, Senator Mullally, deeply devoted to the rule of law and richly schooled in constitutional lore, Holmes, Brandeis, etc., can't wait to tackle those fascinating legal issues, pass on those vitally important judges, lifetime guardians of all our liberties which undergird, etc., etc. Right?" Jerry wrote speeches for me in the '96 and '98 campaigns.

"Right," says Lanny, giving a tomahawk chop with his hand.

I have my elbows on the desk and my head in my hands at this point, but I do manage to give Jerry a little half-wave goodbye as she turns to execute the strategy.

THE ONLY PEOPLE in Washington who get the story more wrong than we did are the ones being paid to get it right, namely, the media. The next morning's page-one treatment by Marian Stultz, the top political reporter in town, contains the following nugget:

> Among those Senators believed to have broken toward Vivian at the last minute are freshmen Raymond Carney of Washington and Terrence Mullally of Massachusetts, both of whom were rewarded with plum committee assignments, on Armed Services and Judiciary respectively.

I am reading this particular item at breakfast when Jerry calls. "Jerry, what did you have to *do* to Marian Stultz to get her to write that? You don't have kids yet, you can't mortgage your firstborn."

"That's what I was calling to say, I didn't have to do anything, not even lie, er, not that I would have, of course. She had the whole thing already written, got it somewhere else or made it up, I just stepped to the side and let her charge by."

"And waved your cape?"

"Well, maybe I wiggled it a little. But you have to keep a straight face and a straight story the next time you see Marian, or she will absolutely torpedo us in the future."

"Consider it done," I say. What the world doesn't know won't hurt them. Or, rather, won't hurt *me.* I have been living by that rule for a long time.

Part Three

So. For the first four months of the session, I was toiling for a majority leader to whom I had given ample grounds for mortal offense. It wasn't until May that my relationship with Anson Vivian took a turn for the better.

From January through April, it was hard to tell which was more dreadful, the leadership of my three committees or the issues.

It was not just Gilliam at Agriculture who was a disaster for me. Vivian made Noel Prudhomme of Louisiana chairman of the Ethics Committee. Senator Prudhomme, a mountainous and ambitious bald man who chewed designer tobacco nonstop, no Red Man for him, understood this to be the punishment it was: he had been Gilliam's whip for southern votes in the majority leader fight. He openly despised me as a northeastern liberal and took pleasure in referring to me as the "gentleman from Massa-Two Shits."

Finally, to the utter surprise of myself and everyone else, Vivian installed himself as chairman of Judiciary, to preside over the two miles of bad road. It was a break with precedent for a majority leader to chair a committee, but his win was so fresh that no one dared buck him, and no one else of stature wanted the job anyway. I decided to keep my head down for a while, and simply stayed away from him.

The issues were no day at the beach either.

Agriculture? First big news story was in February: Wisconsin passes Massachusetts as the number-one cranberry-growing state in the nation. Nice work, Senator Mullally, way to use that clout.

Ethics? We spend ten hours in hearings—remember, the attention span of a United States senator is eight minutes—to decide whether one of our brethren has economized excessively on hotel expenses during trips around the country with female staffers. We vote to issue subpoenas to all the hotels, to see how many rooms were used. Usually—though unfortunately for Senator Fox of Maryland not always—there was a paid-for room in everybody's name. But we couldn't let it go at that, we have to vote to subpoena the *minibar* records of each room. Aha! Gotcha! Senator Fox couldn't have drunk three scotches *and* three vodkas, could he? And Suzie D. *does* drink vodka, according to her girlfriend's exclusive account in the *Examiner.* And there were never any charges to her minibar! And the maid testified that while the coverlet had been thrown back, the bed in Suzie's room did not appear to have been slept in, and none of the towels in the bathroom had been so much as unfolded, though Suzie had removed every single toiletry sample!

Nobody on the committee could have cared less, but we had to fling this dirty laundry out on the line, or the press would have said we didn't care. Which of course was true, we just couldn't have it *said* that we didn't care.

The media were fascinated with the missing toiletries, even though every hotel guest in America palms most every sample in the bathroom. The thumb-sucking analysis was relentless. They couldn't have been used because the towels were dry, and Suzie had no kids to take them home to, she was barely more than a kid herself, a simple cracker kid. It proved too much for Suzie, who tearfully 'fessed up to everything, on national television.

So much for Senator Fox. His wife left him; he declared he would serve out his term, but three days later resigned his seat. Ethics well served all around. The members harrumphed. The remaining members. The surviving members. The members who hadn't yet been caught.

Judiciary? At the outset, Lanny and I hated it for different reasons. Lanny's was political, Happy Gilliam's reason: the issues are controversial, and the losers stay angry, so pretty soon you've offended a majority of your electorate with one vote or another.

I had an additional reason, a personal reason that I kept to myself: I had been an assistant U.S. attorney in Brooklyn for seven years, district attorney in Boston for two, so all the Judiciary Committee staffers wanted me to tell war stories about my experiences as a prosecutor. And there were a number of stories I was not eager to tell, stories that nobody knew, at least nobody who was around now. Nobody who could testify.

■

I F I'D HAD HALF A BRAIN I would have seen in advance what Anson Vivian plainly had seen: that the Judiciary Committee would be ground zero of the increasingly nasty fight between the Senate Democrats and the Republican White House.

The hue and cry for the appointment of independent prosecutors had been somewhat muted during 1998, because the first victim, Commerce Secretary Bob Withers, was a former senator (New Mexico), a former national Republican party chair, and universally known to be a good guy, even if one whose enjoyment of the good life exceeded his means. Deputy Attorney General Simon Buffington, however, was none of these things. The second line on his official résumé proclaimed that he had been Notes and Comment Editor of the *Harvard Law Review*. That went over real big in the Senate. His manner, moreover, was even more supercilious than his résumé. So after the allegations on him hit the papers in April, a number of the members began boning up on the Ethics in Government Act of 1978, as amended. And Anson Vivian didn't have to move an inch. He was right there, as chairman of the relevant committee.

The facts were tangled, the personalities and reactions were not. Former Senator Withers, it was alleged, had accepted luxurious "weekend" hospitality (Thursday to Tuesday) from corporations over whom he had official jurisdiction, both as a senator and as secretary of commerce. Moreover, it was alleged, he had as a senator accepted "speaking" fees on some of these getaways, even when he'd never opened his mouth except to pop in a canapé.

Former Senator Withers, classic stand-up guy, not a defensive bone in his body, admitted all these allegations, did not even bother to point out that everyone else did it and that most lawyers thought it was specifically allowed by the rules governing members of Congress.

Deputy Attorney General Buffington was another kettle of fish.

The deputy attorney general, it had been alleged by anonymous "official sources" in excruciating detail, was the secret beneficial owner of an offshore securities trading account (Grand Caymans) of substantial but indeterminate value, which he had allegedly received as part of a "mutual course of dealing" involving favoritism to certain commercial interests in the discharge of his official duties as deputy attorney general since January 1997.

Deputy Attorney General Buffington responded in the next news cycle in April with a Gatling-gun barrage of denial and accusation. The press was unable to advance the story factually from that point, which confirmed my initial take that the story depended on a singular high-level source.

A source who had now clammed up.

Why? was the question.

No one in Washington thought the rifle shot that had hit Buffington was intended to lodge in his body, to stop at him. Buffington, intellectually able as he was, was the Charlie McCarthy of Harry Frobisch, the attorney general of the United States. And Frobisch's ventriloquist, in turn, was Myron P. Brinker, president of the United States. Both Brinker and Frobisch avoided making any public statement on the Buffington story, other than to say they had complete confidence in him and that the United States Justice Department could handle the matter, indeed had already done so. Never mind how.

What excites the media, and a lot of members of Congress on our side of the aisle, is that Frobisch was Myron Brinker's campaign manager in 1996, and everybody in town knows he has never taken off his campaign hat, even after moving down to Tenth and Constitution. But nobody can prove it.

Harry Frobisch is a piece of work. He's ugly, smart, and smarmy, like a backwater sheriff. Physically he resembles Helmut Kohl, the former German chancellor, except he is even bigger than Kohl. He played halfback at Ohio State—as good as it gets—but unlike most halfbacks, he has run to fat in his middle years, let himself go. All he worries about is covering the ample political backside of his classmate and friend, Myron P. Brinker, who amassed a fortune in the automobile industry—tires, batteries, and accessories—and went on to the governorship and the presidency.

Frobisch doesn't care what anybody thinks about him, and he is very good at what he does. His eyes are always working. He never raises his voice. The guy he most reminds me of, although he's four times his size, is J. Edgar Hoover, whose reign of terror at the FBI spanned almost five decades. Except, I don't think Frobisch is a cross-dresser. He wouldn't be able to find the clothes.

You begin to get the picture, about how the personalities sometimes are less complicated than the facts? That's the backdrop I was operating against, when Anson Vivian came to me on the very first day of May 1999, and strapped me into a bucket on the Washington, D.C., version of the roller coaster.

The difference from regular roller coasters is, in Washington at least somebody gets thrown to their death on every ride.

■

Why was I working on a Saturday afternoon? I have a beautiful young wife, never mind she was toiling away at Johns Hopkins, she needn't have been, we could have been strolling along the old railroad right-of-way in Georgetown.

I was in the bullpen office with Lanny Green and Jerry Traugott, and the door was open, when Anson Vivian walked by at 4:45 fresh from a Law Day speech at American University. He stepped inside, his eyes popping.

"You've got everybody here? What are you, Simon Legree?"

"We in the Northern States don't joke about Simon Legree, Mr. Leader."

"I wasn't with the Rebellion," he deadpanned. "I couldn't have been, I wasn't a state until 1862." Now he laughed. I inferred that his luncheon speech had gone well, or else that he had just corralled a few more likely delegates for the 2000 presidential race.

"Mind if I ask you a question?" he said, indicating my inner office with a jerk of his head. Lanny and Jerry, both dressed in rags, appeared to busy themselves ever more intently about their papers. I knew this meant they were rereading the same line of type a hundred times, devoting all their energies to eavesdropping.

Vivian and I strolled into the inside office. I left the door ajar, he shut it. The humor was gone from his face.

"I bombed at AU today when the print guys were pressing me about exactly why we need independent prosecutors for Withers and Buffington. They won't let me get away with just saying the Justice Department has a conflict of interest. They say, why don't we let DOJ have a swipe at this anyway? Then if they can't make the case, bring in an outside prosecutor. Two bites at the apple, they say."

"What they mean is they've already written 'conflict of interest' 'til they're sick and their editors are on them for another angle."

"Of course that's what they mean. It doesn't mean I don't have a problem. With them."

"You want I should give you the technical reasons?"

"That's why I'm here." He folded his arms. That's supposed to be bad body English, denote hostility, but Anson is enough of a mensch so all it suggested was repose, I am waiting.

I didn't keep him waiting long.

"Four things, if Justice goes first. Each one a deal-breaker. It creates *Brady*, it creates *Jencks*, it creates prior consistents, it can even create complete immunity."

"Okay, I know you know, but I was a civil guy."

"In order to prosecute someone, you have to have evidence, just like in a civil case, except it has to be nine out of ten instead of five point one out of ten. Most of the evidence is statements by witnesses. Okay?"

"You're still speaking my language."

"What the Justice Department has doubtless already done with the Withers case, and what they will do with Buffington if they want to screw it up, is to go and take statements from everybody under the sun, starting with the target, and reduce those to writing."

"Why is that bad?"

"Because the target is the last place you go. You want to negative his avenues of escape first. Otherwise, you have nothing to trip him up with."

"Okay. What's *Brady*?"

"There's a case called *Brady versus Maryland*, you have to turn over to the defense anything that's exculpatory, meaning helpful to the defense in any way. Prior to trial. The test is, if it hurts, it's *Brady* material. These doofuses will go generate a million exculpatory statements from Buffington and all his friends to clog up the record. You don't need that in front of the judge, prior to trial."

"What's *Jencks*?"

"Jencks Act, you got to turn over any prior statements of

any witness you call. They'll go back to any witness who's even slightly adverse to Buffington, interview him exhaustively five times, same subject matter, do FBI three-oh-twos—record of interview—each time."

"Problem?"

"Nobody tells exactly the same story five times. Creates grist for cross-examination. 'How come you forgot this—or, rather, lied about it—in versions two and four?' "

"Okay, I understand there's a problem if it's inconsistent, but why do you say prior consistent is a problem?"

"Because when Buffington or another witness gets on the stand and lies his ass off and you say he just recently made all this up, attack his credibility, he can introduce evidence that he made prior statements consistent with his present lying testimony. It's just something else you don't need in the record. Confuses triers of fact. That's juries. Confuses judges, even."

"Okay, I got it. What's the final thing, the total immunity?"

"We have Colonel Oliver North to thank for that. If Congress immunizes somebody—and Withers and Buffington certainly won't talk to the Hill without it—then they go up there and spill their guts out and they're basically home free on anything they put into the public record. No more two bites: one bite. Forbidden fruit. Adam in the Garden."

"That's the only thing we have to thank Colonel North for."

"I'm with you on that."

"Let me buy you dinner."

■

ANSON VIVIAN'S ORANGE MUSTANG CONVERTIBLE, though parked all day on C Street, had the top down. I guess a Senate plate that reads "1" is a start on a theft insurance policy, in a town with a million Capitol police gumshoes.

He drove us to dinner himself, at considerable speed, and parked in the driveway of a friend on Thirty-first Street, a half block north of M. Almost like Anson has a real life somewhere.

The restaurant he had chosen, Le Canard Enchaîné, has an unusual layout: third floor walk-up, narrow stairs with worn fleurs-de-lis carpeting, no dining room. When you think about it, that's quite a statement for a restaurant to make. Bespeaks a certain confidence. Instead, there are half a dozen studies—faded leather, mahogany, glass decanters lined up on the sideboard. Shabby genteel all the way.

"This was someone's house?"

"Right. Low overhead. Keeps the prices down. Vanessa and I get out of here for less than forty bucks."

A waiter in head-to-toe herringbone stepped from a grouse moor into our doorway, murmuring, "Sorry, gents, I was wondering do you think you would be caring for the venison and wild rice with chestnut purée and boysenberry jam, or the mousseline of pike with celery root and honeyed squash?" He looked vaguely out the window, sorry to have intruded, not wanting to press us.

"One of each," said Senator Vivian without hesitation. The waiter nodded, as though this was a brilliant resolution. Pleased but not surprised.

"And, Andrei?" Vivian continued. The waiter's eyebrows rose expectantly. "A little melted butter on the side."

"Of course, Senator," said our server matter-of-factly.

"Also, for Senator Mullally, a dish of scruples."

"I'm sorry, Senator, I don't believe we have any this evening."

"What?! Have you no scruples?"

"Regrettably not this evening, Senator."

This was evidently a well-worn joke. Neither of them smiled, which made it funnier. Andrei left gratefully.

"Sorry about those scruples," said Vivian.

"Oh, I'll do without." I chuckled.

"Family hold back."

We poured ourselves cocktails into beautiful hand-blown glasses. Vivian took a sip from a glass in the tortured shape of a pickerel, its body so thin that the ice could not sink past the dorsal until it melted to lozenge size. I expected the fish to leap out of his hand at any moment.

He leaned back in his chair.

"You've convinced me we need to stop Harry Frobisch and his Justice Department from trampling on our pea patch."

"Right."

"But the press won't fully buy, unless they get a few more facts to light a fire under Withers or preferably Buffington."

"Right."

"Source of Buffington story has dried up."

"Very obviously."

"Facts adverse to people in power don't surrender themselves voluntarily, or for free."

"Also true. I now see why you are our Leader."

"Ergo, we need to be able to compel the surrender of facts, to help our friends in the media along."

"Sounds logical."

"Sounds to me like you just landed the chairmanship of a new subcommittee, with full power to compel testimony and subpoena documents. Just be careful not to generate any exculpatory material. Or *Jencks.* Or prior consistent statements. Or immunize anybody. I'll notify the press. We'll do an avail at eleven Monday."

I offered my glass in a toast. Vivian's fish rose quickly to the bait, dragging his hand upward.

"I need your expertise and your toughness, Terry. Everybody followed your campaign against Dellenbach, how they went after you, how you gave them the back of your hand. Now you can use my podium. And it won't hurt either of us that Boston TV reaches most of the population of New Hampshire."

I looked Vivian in the eye. "You're not unaware I made a mistake on my first vote in the Senate."

He did not look away. "Everyone makes mistakes in the beginning," he said.

I clinked my glass against the majority leader's pickerel.

"To the work of independent prosecutors, now and forever," I offered blandly. I elected not to include in my toast either of the two slogans that occurred to me: *The higher a monkey climbs on a tree, the more people can see his private parts,* and *Be careful what you wish for.*

◼

THE SWEAT WAS STREAMING off my forehead Monday morning, and it wasn't that hot in the Senate Judiciary Committee hearing room. I knew better than to dab it away with a handkerchief or put my hand to my face. That would be the still photo on page one of every paper and its meaning would be unmistakable: rookie senator can't take the pressure of the big leagues.

Important to look just right. Look attentive—this is important stuff—but not as though you're enjoying yourself. Look as though this is strictly something that has to be done—but not as though you'd rather be anywhere else in the world.

Holding high elective office in our nation's capital really is like having to walk around in a Santa Claus suit, with no beard, all day long, every day of the year. Everybody knows who you are, everybody has standing to jeer at you—except on Christmas—and everybody has an angle.

"I am constrained to say the administration has abused

our patience"—here Anson Vivian caught himself—"the administration has abused the patience of the *American people,* to the point where decisive action is imperative." I nodded. Too lugubriously: a couple of the press guys in the front row smiled. I unpursed my lips just in time, neither one had yet made a note on his pad. That's always a bad sign if they make a note right after they've been looking at you. Like as not, you'll see the word "feign" in their description of you the next day. Or "sheepishly." Or "smirk."

"A majority of the members of the United States Senate Judiciary Committee," Vivian continued, "have now twice requested the appointment of an independent prosecutor to probe apparent wrongdoing—*official* wrongdoing, not personal conduct—on the part of senior members of the Brinker administration. On both occasions, Attorney General Frobisch has denied the request by return mail. So much for the thorough review and investigation required by the statute"— he caught himself again—"required by the *law!*" He shook his jowls. Nice effect. I furrowed my brows in an expression of concern, and snuck a quick peek at the refs in the front row. No more smiles. So far so good.

Vivian was in his glory, and he knew it. Sonorous voice, command of the language. No birdlike air now: he was telling, not asking, doing me the favor of my life and making himself look good in the process. He drew the noose.

"The question is squarely presented whether the refusal of the attorney general to enforce the independent prosecutor law has become itself a violation of that law. Of course, we cannot look to the attorney general for an answer. No one can be a judge in his own cause." Bile rose in my throat, but at least Anson wasn't reading from a text.

"It is for this reason that I must today reluctantly announce the establishment of a new subcommittee, to investigate the operation and execution of the Ethics in Government Act, with full power to compel through subpoena the testimony of witnesses and the production of documents."

Lots of front-row smiles at the word "reluctantly."

"Given the nature of the subcommittee's charge, it is of paramount importance that it be guided by a person of deep experience in the law, and of the highest ethical standards." I allowed my expression to lighten a little, though I could feel the sweat was now beginning to pour freely.

"Not merely a person with an unblemished reputation, but a person whose entire career in office screams integrity." Anson's eyes, everyone's eyes, were on me.

I smiled. Did I hear a faint scream? I thought of my unchallenged reputation for integrity. I thought of sitting on the bed in my one-room apartment in Brooklyn ten years earlier, counting out the twenties and fifties. Terrence Mullally, Jr., assistant U.S. attorney, United States Department of Justice, counting out ninety thousand dollars in small bills. All mine.

"So I give you now a man new to the Senate but long experienced in the law, that veteran state and federal prosecutor, the chairman of our new investigative subcommittee, Senator Terrence Mullally of Massachusetts!" Hearty applause from the staffers, they knew CNN and C-SPAN were going live and couldn't edit it out. Press pencils poised.

I stepped smartly forward. I made the mistake of focusing on a man in the third row. Something in the angle of the jaw . . . He turned into Rudy Solano. My eyes blurred. He became Detective Lieutenant Rudy Solano, pitching awkwardly, putting out his arm, falling and sinking in the snow, in a growing eddy of blood.

Freshman error. Don't look at an individual face, look over the heads of the back row. Focus on your message, not your audience. Stay on message.

I recovered by staring at a light on the back wall, then beamed at Senator Vivian and placed my fingers lightly, confidently, on either side of the podium. No notes required. No notes ever required in the big leagues. This is the Show.

"You are too kind, Mr. Majority Leader," I said.

In truth, he had been considerably too kind. But neither Anson Vivian nor anyone else in Washington, D.C., knew that. Two men had known it, two police officers, but they were both dead. And one crook. One Chinese bad boy whom we had let walk away. But I had never met him and he had never met me.

All I had to do was act natural.

I knew the subcommittee's real job was to destroy Myron Brinker's administration and everything in it, root and branch, so in my remarks I sought to convey the opposite impression—namely, that ours was a scholarly venture, lots of interesting legal questions, certainly no belligerence, no prejudgment.

The press troops all had handheld recorders whirring, nobody needed to write down a word I said. Instead, they were staring at me intently. Their pencils were to be used only to write down mistakes or inconsistencies. Or, better still, disagreements. A couple of the tough-guy types, their ties already at half-mast at eleven in the morning, seemed to be trying to make their watery eyes blaze at me. The effort failed.

I kept my game face on, so even if they suspected I didn't believe a word I was saying—and I'm sure they did—they couldn't prove it through me. I spoke only two and a half minutes. Don't gild the lily when things are breaking your way. As I yielded the mike, I could see in Vivian's eyes that I had done well to keep it short, keep the mood upbeat.

As long as you keep a straight face, they have to report what you say. Especially the electronic media, TV and radio, because they need your image or voice to prove they're authentic. The print folks have more editorial latitude, can garble your message by putting it in indirect discourse instead of quoting you, basically make you look like a drooling idiot if they want to. I don't know whether they're more skeptical because they have the power to be dangerous, or more dangerous because they're more skeptical. But they're definitely both.

What I wanted to talk to the media about that morning was precisely nothing. Not my glittering résumé, which could only get duller on inspection; not my coy plans, which could only seem less noble if they were fleshed out. So as Vivian pointed to the first questioner, I took not one but four steps to my right, which brought me to the side door of the hearing room.

There I was intercepted by a gaggle of touring schoolgirls.

Ordinarily I would have pressed past them—they were obviously from the Midwest, probably Farm Belt—but on this occasion, I saw opportunity in their upturned shining faces. An opportunity for shelter, that is, from further examination by a possibly frustrated press corps. I indicated to their teacher, a young red-cheeked brunette with even white teeth, that I would be more than thrilled to talk with the girls just outside in the hall, so as not to disturb the important proceedings. Just on the other side of that door.

Click. Sometimes the sweetest sound.

"Senator, I'm from Chillicothe, Ohio!"

"Oh, yes, that was your state's first capital, was it not?" I had studied up on Ohio during Brinker's presidential campaign. Know your enemy.

"Yes, and I'm from Bucyrus, home of President Brinker and the biggest bratwursts in the *whole world!*"

One and the same, I thought. I smiled at the young lady. "So I understand," I said enthusiastically.

"So, have you actually *met* President Brinker, Senator?"

"Oh yes, he's, he's quite a, a, quite a guy."

"We'll tell him we saw you when we go to his party at Christmas," she declared forthrightly.

"Please do!"

I wouldn't want to be a fly on the wall at that social event. That's eight months from now, we may have half his inner circle under indictment or otherwise ruined by then.

"It was nice meeting you, Senator. You're from Maryland, aren't you?"

"Massachusetts." My warmest smile.

"Oh! Sorry!"

"Not at all, Maryland's a great state. So's Ohio." I gave a little wave, to punctuate this exit line.

I found myself alone, blissfully alone, in the corridor and moved along rapidly, head down, so the press wouldn't catch up with me. In the safety of the chairman's hideaway office, I shook my head from side to side: those girls had absolutely no idea what they had witnessed in the hearing room. Next year,

Miss Poppins should take them to Africa, on safari: maybe there they would at least recognize the savagery.

■

THAT NIGHT AS WE LAY IN BED, Emma stroked my neck. I was completely relaxed.

"You were good on TV today," she said.

"I know," I said.

"There's something you should know," she said.

Every muscle in my neck and arms went taut.

"What's that?"

"I woke up that night, Terry. Wine and stingers may put me down, but they won't keep me out. I was just having a little nap, is all."

"Woke up? What night?"

"The night you drove up to Jaffrey in the snow, when you thought I was passed out, the night Rudy supposedly shot himself, but didn't."

"You're telling me? I was the *only* one who testified I didn't think it was sui—"

She patted my arm.

"Yes, I know, and I admired you for it, it must have been very hard for you—all those tears at the coroner's inquest, especially. It was a great performance."

I stared at Emma.

"Don't calculate, Terry. Don't try to bullshit me now, or you'll ruin everything. No more secrets, okay? We've already been through this once. You promised me no secrets when I moved my stuff in to Commonwealth Avenue, and in no time you were living a lie, acting out a lie. The only reason I let you go on was you were obviously doing it to protect what we had together, so it was in my interest as well as yours."

"Mind if I have a cigarette?"

"Help yourself." She had to notice my hand was shaking.

Emma rubbed the knuckles of my other hand. This was more calming than a kind word. If I have to deal with someone in a crisis, let it be a woman and not a man.

She gently took my chin in her hand and turned my head so I had to look at her.

"Don't worry," she said. "I'm not even unhappy about what happened, or at least what I think happened. I always thought Rudy was a poisonous snake. I hated what he did to you, the way you acted around him.

"You think I didn't know he had something hanging over your head? You're not that good an actor, Terry. The days before Rudy fetched up dead in the snow, you couldn't even pronounce his name in a normal voice."

"I didn't realize it showed," I said.

"That's why I'm telling you now," she said. "I almost told you the other night, when you were moaning about Rudy in your sleep. Rudy and Happy Gilliam.

"It's not good for you, of all men, Terry Mullally, to think you're fooling people. I know sometimes you do, but not as often as you think. You think you're taking advantage of Sarah Blakeslee and Happy Gilliam, for example? Hardly. You're the ingenue here, not them.

"You're fighting a two-front war, your past and your present, all by yourself. I'm afraid it's going to chew you up."

The floor fell away. Of course, there was nothing I could say. My wife knew I had killed a man and covered it up, had known for years. I felt pressed down, naked, helpless, the way I had felt at the orphanage.

After years of posing as the inevitable and indestructible man, it was an exhilarating feeling.

Part Four

I HAD NO DREAMS THAT NIGHT, but my subconscious must have been working overtime to make adjustments for my new situation, because I woke up exhausted. I had a lot of changes to make in my script, internal and external.

I knew I had to puff myself up and go back to work at the most exclusive club in the world, but my rhythms were off. The normal bravura, which covers the gaps and the unexpected, was missing. I forgot to pick up a eucalyptus nut on my way to the car. When I got to the office, I wondered whether a guard would ask to see the eucalyptus fruit, with the little *Y* in it.

One of the first people I saw in the corridors of Hart was Happy Gilliam. He gave me a passable wave hello, but his eyes said, *I heard what you said to Anson: "I made a mistake on my first vote in the Senate."* Or did they? He was by me now, downriver. You never step into the same stream twice, in Washington.

This man came within three votes of being elected majority leader, I said to myself. This man is the chairman of the Democratic Senatorial Campaign Committee, controlling the purse, and chairman of the Agriculture Committee, controlling where you sit and what you get to read and vote on. You told his rival that you made a mistake in voting for him. And they've known each other for twenty years, and talk for two hours every day, so maybe your little secret isn't so secret.

I sat hunched behind my massive walnut desk, elbows on the glass, head sunk in my hands, and decided it was time to invite Happy Gilliam and his wife to Olive Street for a weekend dinner. You never know where your next coalition might be coming from.

That evening, Emma proved resistant to the idea.

"Because he's dangerous to you, or because he's so incomprehensible to you? I don't get it. Neither one's a good reason."

I took a breath. Best not to join issue here. Logic would not be on my side.

"I'm willing to pay dearly for this," I said. "You can have anybody else you want."

"I'll want Ruthie Truslow, for openers."

I groaned. Ruth Truslow was a naughty schoolmate of Emma's from Boston who had bummed around the world for years and only recently graduated from college. She was known for force of personality and bad taste. Her nickname was the Human Tornado.

"I love Ruthie, but you don't think Happy might carry her off in the middle of dinner? Would be awkward."

"Ruthie can take care of herself. Besides, she's the one who got me into anthropology in the first place. She's been to all these places I'm reading about. It won't be dull, if I can coax her down from New York."

"Yes, that's what I was afraid of. I was afraid it would be dull."

Emma jabbed her elbow into my ribs to reward me for my humor.

"Also, I want both Lanny and Jerry. Invite them for a full hour earlier than the Gilliams to get me in a good mood."

On the appointed Sunday, dinner was called for seven. Ruthie Truslow, only too happy to jump on the Delta shuttle, told Emma she would have in tow "a struggling lawyer named Fenster." I guessed, correctly, that this would be Tom Fenster, a former U.S. Supreme Court law clerk who was now in meteoric ascent at a powerhouse Democratic law firm on K Street. To round out the party, Jerry Traugott had suggested it would be "good for business" to ask Marian Stultz of the *Tribune*.

Lanny arrived at five-thirty, per Emma's instructions. He had—how shall I say this?—ample luggage under his eyes for a lengthy stay on Olive Street. Long Saturday night, it looked like. Gave Emma a peck on the cheek, did not look at me, and flung himself onto the window seat, a man with no edge.

"Coffee, double strength?"

"How did you guess." For the next several minutes, he groaned in counterpoint to my disapproving Silex.

"You two sound like the Budweiser toads," Emma volunteered.

"Frogs," moaned Lanny miserably, without opening his mouth.

I offered a glass mug of espresso, which was manfully sipped down. We waited. No effect. Lanny wasn't really even sitting on the window seat, truth be told, just situated on it, like a beanbag.

Emma smiled and shook her head, "Tsk, tsk!" She surveyed him.

"Lanny, my dearest, Terry's stupid coffee is not doing *it* for you, whatever *it* is; you don't need coffee, you need a *cigarette*, or two or three. *And* I know just where they are, I hid them in the kitchen, right near the food supply, where no one would ever think to look." She pivoted, disappeared, and reentered.

Lanny Green increased in stature, rose without moving, acquired angles, elbows. He fairly flung his mug onto the sill as a useless crutch. Now—I was spellbound—now he did rise, and extended a fluid and graceful hand. Graceful but unmistakably prehensile. From behind me appeared an answering arm, a fistful of nonfilter Camels, another hand proffering a book of Ohio bluetip matches, finally the full figure of my wife.

Lanny's thumb and forefinger closed on two of the Camels. He lit them with no wasted motion and inhaled deeply. He closed his eyes.

Emma folded her arms and leaned back against the wall, beaming at her handiwork.

"Addiction is a beautiful thing," she said.

Lanny opened his eyes. The strain was gone. He looked straight at me, impatiently, and tapped both cigarettes in the general direction of my wood duck ashtray. The embers fell on our only Persian rug, price fifty-five hundred dollars. I restrained myself.

"Okay, Boss, let's get going. Staff screwed up the memo in the daily binder on Thursday and you voted wrong on that procedural issue, campaign finance reform. Opposite of what we had already said. Press knows, is puzzled. What can we say tonight? Can't hide here, can't even run. Card-carrying VC coming."

"VC?" from Emma.

"Vietcong. That's what Lanny calls reporters."

"Why, because they all wear black pajamas at night and would as soon kill you as look at you?"

"Right."

"Hmm," hmmed Emma. "How about, 'Mistakes were made'? Has a certain historical ring to it . . ."

Lanny shook his head in disgust. "Much too straightforward. Points right at us."

"How about, 'Mistakes made themselves'?" I suggested.

"Much better, much better." Lanny inhaled thoughtfully. He was comfortable now. Emma smiled at him.

"I hope you guys know where the line is, the edge."

"We do, we do, at least we can see it coming," said Lanny.

Emma didn't seem convinced.

Jerry Traugott walked in at ten of six, through the front hall and living room right into the kitchen, click click, fishnet stockings, sort of nodded but didn't say hello to anybody. I love Jerry. You know what she is? There's only one word for it. She's a dame. She used to be a gossip columnist, told me once there's only three things that are important, sex, money, and liquor, and any one of the three will get you the other two.

Pop! From the kitchen.

"Isn't it a bit early for the shampers, J.T.?" called Lanny without looking up from the current *Cook's Political Report*.

"Recovering alcoholic," said Jerry, appearing with a water

glass full of champagne. She was not explaining, merely announcing herself, grand entrance.

"Recovering from last night?" Lanny was yawning. This is going to be a hell of a dinner party, I thought.

"Right." Slurp.

Lanny seemed glad to see Jerry. He absentmindedly kissed her on the forehead—a big "smooch"—then buried his face in the back of her neck.

"Ahh, Niki de Saint Phalle. You positively mos' compellin' woman I know."

Jerry shut her eyes. She had on a white sweater with vertical ribs. When Lanny nuzzled her, she arched her back, and both nipples showed through the sweater. I slipped through the double doors into the dining nook and busied myself studying a wall map of seventeenth-century Manhattan. This all happened very fast. I knew one thing, I wasn't leaving that map unless I was invited to.

I snuck a peek into the living room. Lanny had sat down and was back deep in his *Cook's Political Report.* Jerry had moved around behind him, was running her fingers through the hair on the back of his neck.

"That tickles, stop that," he mumbled. He was reading with difficulty, with his finger. "Hey, look, that race in New Jersey is tightening!"

"You're supposed to say, 'That tickles, keep doing that,' you idiot." Jerry was at least straightforward.

"Oh. Yeah it does, it feels, it feels . . . fine. Good. Oh God, we're going to lose Virginia."

From above and behind, Jerry struck the periodical from his grasp with a vicious chop of her right hand.

Lanny looked up with his mouth open. He was not computing. "What, what did you do that for?"

Maybe I watched too much daytime TV at the foster home in Brooklyn when I was a teenager: I thought Jerry T. should have burst into tears at this point. She elected not to sully her professional standing, however, and merely marched out of the room. My wife, her face set, glided after her into the kitchen. A four-masted schooner under full sail, Emma would have crushed anything in her path.

Lanny Green, the smartest person I know, was shaking his head, muttering, "Geez," and bending to the task of reassembling his *Cook's Political Report*.

I edged back through the double doors. "Nice work, soldier," I said.

"Hey, listen, sure, I know. One sex takes out the garbage, the other shops. Great. *Vive la différence.* We don't watch it, we *are* going to lose Virginia. Again! No excuse for that."

Whew. No accounting for taste. Those nipples have stayed with me. I can't get them off the inside of my eyelids. If I was in charge of strategy, we'd probably keep on losing Virginia.

■

AT THREE MINUTES PAST SEVEN, Emma opened the door to Happy and Mona Gilliam. Senator Gilliam kissed her hand—just the tips of her fingers. So, I figure, his radar wasn't entirely off when Emma was studying the ceiling at the Pied de Mouton.

Mona Gilliam looked like Harriet in *Ozzie and Harriet*, the 1950s TV show, except her hair was white. She'd obviously had a permanent that afternoon. Shrank the size of her head by half. Most unfortunate. The word around town was she was another of those women whom a successful politician had married too early.

Goes to show you what the word around town knows. Mona had barely set foot in the house before marching over to a bookcase and removing two adjoining books.

"Can't have these together, I'm afraid," she said, handing them to Emma. "Neither would approve."

Emma looked down. One book was Freud, the other Nabokov. "Omigosh, you're *right!*" she exclaimed. "The *movers* must have done that!"

Good laugh all around. Things were getting off on the right foot. We escorted the Gilliams into the living room, where Lanny and Jerry, to my amazement, were standing by the fire talking to each other, almost like grown-ups.

Senator Gilliam obviously had some difficulty as a result of Jerry's sweater, but did manage to bring Mona front and center and introduce her.

"How *nice* to see you," said Mona easily. "And tell me, where are you living? Have you taken a place in the District, to be near the office?"

"Yes, I was in close to work, but I'm actually moving tomorrow," Jerry explained nervously, suddenly seeming very young. "From a basement apartment on the Hill to a studio off Calvert Street, in Adams-Morgan. Right near Madam's Organ. You know, the bluegrass place. The timing was perfect because I've just used up the last of my shampoo and my mouthwash, so I don't have to move small amounts of either of them. *Or* pour them in the sink. So, it worked out great!" She cracked her knuckles.

"I see," said Mrs. Gilliam, arching her eyebrows.

"Adams-Morgan can be a dangerous neighborhood, Miz Truzlow. I hope you have a doorman in your building, to protect you," said Senator Gilliam.

"No, there's no doorman in the whole neighborhood. You can come and go whenever you want. By the way, I pronounce it 'Truss-low,' as in, tie up a wolf. That's what the name comes from."

Happy Gilliam nodded. Mona Gilliam choked on something.

"Happy!" I put in quickly. "What can I get you to drink?"

"Oh, I'll follow you," he drawled. "What's for dinner?"

"Shad and shad roe, slab bacon, lots of lemon, Vidalia onions, snow peas, new potatoes, celery braised in sugar water, beefsteak tomatoes, all one course.

"Sounds like you gave Mrs. Mullally the night off," said Mona Gilliam. "That's a man's cooking, a big man's cooking."

"I sliced the tomatoes!" said Emma.

"It's the cooking of a man after my own heart," said Happy seriously, patting the middle button of his suede vest.

My chef's ego stoked, I left Lanny and Emma to attend to the drinks and made my way into the kitchen, where I donned my cream-colored apron. It bore evidence of many dishes, sauces, and vintages.

I looked around. I was glad to be alone. The kitchen was ridiculously small. Also, when you're trying to make seven things come out at the same time, with a stove that has one oven and four crummy electric burners, you don't want any witnesses to the fevered Marx Brothers juggling of saucepans and fry pans. The shad and onions were okay in the oven, but the roe, bacon, snow peas, potatoes, and celery had to play musical burners. Just not senatorial, so we don't need a gallery.

I was minding my own business, not to be confused with sampling the fattest pieces of bacon, when I heard laughing and clinking, followed by the unwelcome creak of the swinging door.

"Honey, you know Marian Stultz from the *Tribune!*"

I tried to hide the bacon before turning around and forcing a smile.

"Oh, hi!"

Marian reached for my hand. Was the bacon still there? I didn't dare look down. Taking a chance, I shook her hand, and was relieved not to see her face freeze in horror.

"Marian and I just wondered if we could, you know, just sort of, *help*," Emma simpered. She was busting my chops. She knows damn well I hate company when I'm preparing a meal.

"Out! Out of my kitchen!" I screamed. "I can't concentrate! Women weaken cooks!"

"I thought that was legs, dear," said Emma over her shoulder.

"Legs and cooks. Point is, *Raus raus, lass mich doch in Ruhe!*" This means "leave me alone" in German and it's not polite. There are lots of things I like to say in German. When they were safely out of range, I brandished a butcher's knife after them to reinforce my joke.

Just then—must he always choose the most unlucky moment for an entrance?—Happy Gilliam pushed through the swinging door into the kitchen. The blade of my butcher knife would have cleaved his forehead in two if I had advanced it a foot. We both stared at the knife, as though it were an alien arrival unconnected to either of us. I let it sink, and hooked my thumbs into the sides of my apron, to show I was at my ease. The butcher knife dangled by its thong from my wrist.

Not even a collegiate performance, really, let alone postgrad. I was glad the younger crowd hadn't seen.

Gilliam, perfectly relaxed, moved past me as though nothing was out of the ordinary. He went to the cupboards above the sink. He allowed an expression of concern only when he pretended he couldn't find what he wanted.

"Senator, if I may, where are the bitters?"

The Angostura bitters were in the back of the cupboard and obviously Happy had seen them or he wouldn't have said, "Where are the . . ." he would have said, "Do you by any chance have any?" And he knew a conversational exchange of some sort was necessary to put the awkwardness behind us. My opinion of Harlan Gilliam was rising.

"They're right there at the back, Mr. Chairman," I offered helpfully, stowing the butcher knife on a counter.

"Ohh, of course!" His hand clapped the broad forehead so nearly cloven.

In a single motion, he took two sugar cubes from our Wyler's bowl, applied four drops of Angostura, and dropped the freighted cargo into his old-fashioned glass. There didn't appear to be much water, even frozen water, with the bourbon.

I saw Emma had given him two maraschino cherries. Bet he didn't have to ask for them.

Gilliam took a sip from the dark semiviscous mass, wiped the back of his hand across his mouth, and made a guttural noise suggesting pleasure.

"That's balm for the spirit." He sighed, looking not at me but at the swinging door to the dining room.

"You are good to have us all," he added, still looking at the door, as though he were afraid a wild beast might burst through at any moment.

Now he turned to address me directly, in a low, urgent voice.

"Senator, we didn't have an opportunity to finish our conversation in the hall outside my office the other day. I wanted to clarify what was said about receiving support through a variety of channels."

Oh, boy, here comes the trimming and wiggling out. *What was said*—not even *what I said*. He must have talked to a campaign finance lawyer since my last encounter with the Rockette in Chief, Sarah Blakeslee.

"Not at all, Mr. Chairman. I think it's well known there's only one proper cha—"

"On the contrary." He moved closer to me, holding his hammered glass before him slightly aloft, as though it contained a sacrament and I was about to be initiated into a mysterious rite. I am Jesuit-trained: should I reach behind me for a wafer and dip it in his goblet? He seems bent on something, better sit tight.

"I wanted you to have the benefit of my experience." His face was now closer to mine than is polite in normal conversation. On the bridge of his nose I saw two scars I had not noticed before. Put there generations ago by a dying cowboy, perhaps.

"So many men come to Washington feeling they must take a vow of poverty to please their enemies"—here he glanced at the door again—"with the result that they wind up placing enormous pressures on themselves, constraining their freedom of action. I fear the public good is often the ultimate loser, in such circumstances."

This was so far from politically correct that it appealed to the contrarian strain in me. "I don't believe in vows of poverty," I said brightly.

"I thought not." He put a hand on my shoulder. "May I tell you something, strictly off the record, you and me only?"

"Certainly, Mr. Chairman. If it's not off the record in this town, it's barely worth hearing."

"Occasionally, there are opportunities to get in on the ground floor in pooled investments, nothing short-swing, investments for the longer term, handled always by reputable professionals. The returns, after a period of three or four years, can be quite handsome."

"Just in time for the reelect."

"This isn't for your reelection campaign, this is for you, so you don't have to constantly worry and rush around making speeches for five hundred dollars, so you can take your time and make up your own mind on the issues, on the merits."

I smiled at his artlessness. Or was it artfulness? For no reason at all I thought of Emma, swinging in our hammock, one leg crooked over the side, staring at the sky. No reason but core values. Leisure. Money.

"What sort of investments?"

"Oh, for example, commodity pools. It's a tricky and difficult business, which is why you wouldn't want to get near the day-to-day decision-making, better to be a million miles away, as investors customarily are in these things."

"How much of an initial investment is required?"

"Generally fifty to a hundred thousand dollars."

"I have two mortgages, I don't have fifty thousand dollars to spare."

Gilliam studied me for a moment.

"Yes you do," he said. "I've discussed it with Miss Blakeslee's people."

We stared at each other. Gilliam took a slow sip of his Manhattan. I nodded.

"I'm glad to hear that," I said.

Gilliam smiled. Triumphantly?

I stared at him.

"Give it some thought, anyway," he concluded, his voice rising to a normal tone. "No paperwork required, at this time." He pushed through the swinging door, bellowing "Ladies!" to the company in the next room. The door swung shut.

No paperwork required at this time. I wonder when the managers of the pool determine which investors have done extremely well and which have been not quite so fortunate.

At the end of every trading day?

Or, perhaps more likely, at the end of four years, when the pool winds up its affairs? Nothing officially realized until then, no gains, no losses.

Senator, surprise! You did great! Here are all your trading records so you can declare your income and it's all perfectly legal! Your fifty grand, which we stood you on spec, is now worth over two million!

I smiled and shook my head. My opinion of Harlan Gilliam was falling. *So you can take your time and make up your own mind on the issues, on the merits.* What a butter-and-egg man, what a smoothie. What a joke. The public corruption unit of the United States attorney's office in Brooklyn had prosecuted similar cases twice while I was there, once as bribery and once as stock market manipulation. I knew far too much to get roped into this.

Wait. What had I said, exactly? Had I said anything? Had I been daydreaming about the money, the promise of ease with Emma? I should say something . . .

An ugly hiss made me jump and turn to face it.

The saucepan with the snow peas was boiling over. Can't have that, those babies overcook and go limp in about two minutes.

As I attended again to my duties, my opinion of myself had fallen. Maybe seven dishes and a course in avarice is more than I can handle at one time.

■

I ARRANGED THE SHAD, ROE, bacon, and onions on our one enormous china serving dish, which was inappropriately painted with a Thanksgiving turkey. Must get more serving dishes. Must get bigger kitchen, two ovens, six burners, more counter space.

High chatter from beyond the swinging door. Evidently, the Human Tornado had touched down at Olive Street.

I stuck my head out to announce all was in readiness. Ruth Truslow, in designer red satin, threw her arms around my neck and kissed me on the lips. Tasty, I have to say.

"Terry, you look so senatorial in that apron! What have you been killing out there?"

"My tuxedo's at the cleaner's. Is that Gotham roughwear you have on?"

"Darling, I always wear black tie to dinner parties, so I can say I'm going on to some Arab's birthday bash if things get slow, you and Ems know that."

"How was your flight?"

"Heavenly. The best part is those metal detectors. They ding me every time, and I love the scanners, they tickle so much. I always ask for the male scan."

Happy Gilliam left his wife talking to Tom Fenster and strolled over to us.

"Don't you take off those bracelets?"

"Every night, Senator. And also at the airport."

Happy looked her up and down. There was not a lot he couldn't see, and no metal apparent but the bracelets.

"But you always set off the machine?"

Ruthie batted her eyes at him.

"Navel ring, Senator."

A vein appeared on Happy's forehead. He looked at the floor.

"Soup's on!" I shouted.

I seated Happy Gilliam as far away from Ruthie as I could. I was to regret this maneuver, as it placed him in the company of Marian Stultz. Our dining nook was a jungle that night.

Jerry Traugott called across the table to Ruthie, "Are you working in the city, or studying, or hanging out?"

"Hanging out. I just finished college, believe it or not, age twenty-eight, may go on to grad school."

"What would be your field?" asked Mona Gilliam.

"I'm an expert in sex."

"Sects?"

"Sex."

"Oh, is that so?" Mona had to reach for a glass of water to keep her food down.

"Yes. Well, I'm not a professional like dear Ems here"— Emma blushed at this, I am quick to report—"I mean, I'm not enrolled in a Ph.D. program or anything, but I'm thinking maybe of a master's at NYU next year, either anthropology or biology. Plant sex, insects, birds, primates, maybe Pygmies or headhunters."

Lanny's forehead was wrinkled. He was concentrating hard, to no avail.

"Plant sex?"

"It's the most interesting of all," said Ruthie, "the most willful and also the most skillful, because they can't, you know, move around."

"No, they're kind of—" Tom Fenster, at the top of his profession, was waving his right hand in little circles, trying to conjure up a word—"rooted to the spot." Now his color deepened. Order of the Coif, and floundering. The Human Tornado does that to people.

"Exactly right," said Ruthie, "so they grow their flowers perfectly crimson"—a sidelong glance at Fenster here—"to attract the bees and hummingbirds who carry the pollen to a flower of the opposite sex, on another tree."

"Like go-betweens carrying lovers' letters, in days of yore," Emma suggested.

"Just so. And the female plants won't accept pollen unless it's from a male flower, and it has to be from the same kind of tree, no miscegenation, but a different tree."

"Scient insect, no incest," said Emma.

Ruthie nodded approvingly, but clearly didn't want to be headed off, even by a triple anagram. "Then there are less parentally responsible plants like grasses," she hurried on, "which use wind to broadcast their seed. They don't care where it goes, they just want it out there in quantity."

"Interesting," said Happy Gilliam.

"The big debate now is about insects, moths and fruit flies particularly. The question is, why do the males have such fancy genitalia?"

"*Is* it?" said Tom Fenster, a picture of confusion.

"The traditional explanation was called 'lock and key': had to make sure it was the right fit, that guaranteed it was the right species or subspecies and not some impostor."

"What's the current thinking?" I asked.

"People have been noticing, a lot of these hairy whirls and orbs never get near penetrating the female, they just tickle her belly during coitus. So the new theory is called 'female preference.' They've proved it by studies of female flies and moths who mate more than once, with more than one partner. They go for the guys who tickle them."

"Why can't lock and key and female preference both be true?" asked Fenster, grateful to have spotted an issue.

"Could be, for the fruit flies," said Ruthie with a little sniff. She was evidently not bowled over by her date's issue-spotting ability. "But not too much higher up the chain. Female preference in humans, for example, obviously goes well beyond lock and key." She put her napkin in Fenster's hand. Either she had gotten that from Emma, or Emma had picked it up from her.

"Birds?" I asked.

"I studied the painted snipe and the bronze-winged jacana," said Ruthie. "The males incubate and raise the chicks, and every female has a harem of males that she visits regularly."

"What do you think about the 'demonic male' theory?" asked Emma. "You know, we're all descended from killer apes and big-game hunters, so female hominids and humans will select the raging guy because he's the best breadwinner, male selects the prettiest and most passive female, then kills her young to bring her back into oestrus so he can sire a new brood on her?"

"Complete horseshit. Moronic males, is closer to it. If violence in humans came from killer apes, you'd see dented skulls and multiple arm fractures much earlier. They don't really show up much until the Neolithic period."

"What about the animules in Raymond Dart's cave, with *Australopithicus?*" said Emma. "They say that proves it."

"I've been to that cave and I've seen those bones. It was a leopard den, or hyenas, maybe, and that young *Australopithicus* wasn't eating anything. He got *et.* The claw marks are right there on the bones."

"I thought they also based this on a study of the chimpanzees at Gombe," said Emma.

"A study guaranteed to skew the results, because the anthropologists introduced a centralized food supply. If the food is scattered, as in nature, there's not so much competition and anxiety. Provisioning creates intensified violence. The watcher messes up what she's watching."

I looked at Lanny, then at Emma.

"Chimp rules," said Lanny. Emma and I laughed.

"Plus," Ruthie went on relentlessly, "half the infanticides at Gombe were done by *females!* Men and women are simply not that different in times of stress. Males and females, they all have it in them."

I was thinking, maybe I should bum around the world for six years. I looked down the table at Gilliam. His mouth was open. He was looking at the wall.

"Then, finally, I've done a little work with South American

tribes," Ruthie concluded. "I was actually with the *Bari* in the Venezuelan rain forest for a month and a half. They're more advanced than we are, they observe polyandry or 'partible paternity.' Any man who sleeps with a woman before or during her pregnancy—and they're pregnant or nursing almost all the time, as long as they're fertile—is regarded as contributing to the fetus and so has an obligation to help support the mother and child."

"Barbaric," said Happy Gilliam, patting his mouth with his napkin.

"Each to his own," said Ruthie.

■

I WAS ON THE POINT OF KNOCKING OVER a glass of Australian red wine so as to change the subject, but Marian Stultz saw an opening and came to the rescue.

"So, Senator Gilliam," she said thoughtfully, "tell me, it must be fascinating, getting to meet so many new people while you're doing the fund-raising for your presidential campaign?" Her mouth was pursed, tiny eyebrows arched expectantly. Everyone was quiet.

Marian lowered her voice, ensuring universal attention. "I understand from a new staffer at the Democratic Senatorial Campaign Committee that you raised almost two million dollars last month. That must be some kind of a record! And I looked and looked at all the reports and I couldn't make it add up to two million. All I found was a million and a quarter!"

Someone got caught with a mouthful of water and swallowed audibly. I didn't turn to look.

Make that a very new staffer at the Campaign Committee, I thought, a soon-to-be-former staffer.

Then I had another thought, a chilling thought.

Opportunities in pooled investments.

"What I can't figure out is why I can't make the figures match."

Tricky and difficult business.

"Meaning, you know, where I should look."

Better to be a million miles away, as investors customarily are.

Could Marian have listened at the door, overheard us? No, voices too low. Besides, everyone else would have seen her. And swinging doors don't have keyholes. Or do they?

Would Happy blame me for this inquiry, think this was a setup? Would he blow up on the witness stand?

I need not have worried on the last point. Happy was the picture of bemused relaxation as he came right back at Marian with magnolia, suffocating magnolia.

"Whaa Miz Stultz, I'm happy to hear we're doin' well, but I'm not surprazz. I get a good response out there around the country to our message, so I'm sure folks do want to spoat me. As for those re-poats, I leave them to the loys and accountants, but I'd be very surprazz if we're not fully in compliance. Whatever folks are good enough to give us, and I have no idea of the totals, it's all right in there."

Good parry. No factual assertions for her to tear apart. Gilliam must be sweating it, though. Glad it's not me she's after.

Wait.

I don't have fifty thousand dollars. Yes you do, I've discussed it. I'm glad to hear that.

Oh God. Marian, this is *my house,* for pity's sake. Mercifully, Marian offered no resistance when Ruthie Truslow clanked her fork down and butted in.

"Senator"—munch munch munch—"please pardon my ignorance"—now and only now she finished her mouthful—"but how would you describe that message you're giving to folks around the U.S. of A.? What is that message?"

Gilliam snorted, swallowed onions and potatoes, wiped his face again, and grinned good-naturedly, raising his glass to Ruthie: *"In vino veritas."*

"Isn't that the Harvard message, I mean the Harvard motto?" suggested Tom Fenster.

Gilliam roared. "Oh, that's a good one, Tom, that's a good one! Don't you think, Mona?"

End of topic. Marian Stultz busied herself about her food and did not look up.

Toward the close of the meal, Fenster brought us back to the presidential race, but took care not to aim a shaft anywhere near his fellow Democrat Happy Gilliam.

"Raise your hands, everyone who believes Myron Brinker will stick to his plan to serve only one term."

Not a hand at the table moved. Georgetown dinner parties were not exactly the president's political stronghold.

"Raise your hands," Fenster continued, "everyone who

thinks Myron Brinker is glad he picked Martha Holloway to run with him." Again, no movement. Holloway was as dynamic as Brinker was dull.

"No room for gratitude in politics," Fenster remarked. "Campaign Manager Frobisch froze her out the day after the election. What's your take on her, Senator?"

"I'm not a good person to ask," I said, "because I'm prejudiced in her favor on account of she grew up on a cattle ranch and I hear she's handy with a gun."

"Straight shooter in politics, too," said Marian Stultz. "That's why Frobisch can't stand her, he likes to play hide-the-ball, keep everybody guessing, with her it's all out in the open." She looked around: oops, she had dropped her mask of witlessness. But not to worry, we weren't buying anyway.

"If he's so stupid," interposed Mona Gilliam, "how come he got that tire salesman elected president of the United States?"

Gilliam winced. "Now, Mona . . ."

"I'm serious, it has nothing to do with style. It's the clash of the tectonic plates: her crime is she's forty-seven, she's ambitious, and she has a good relationship with the national press corps. If that old fart keeps his pledge not to run again—which I am far from saying there is any chance of his doing—she'll run in a minute."

This is the woman Happy Gilliam married too early?

Over the brandy, Marian Stultz called down the table to me, "Have you heard about your boy coming to town, Senator?"

"No, what?"

"Your fellow marksman Ms. Holloway finally won a big one. She got one of her guys appointed head of the Criminal Division at Justice, now U.S. attorney in Boston, hard charger, used to work for you, name of Sacco."

"Vacco? Phil Vacco is going to be the head of the Criminal Division?"

"Yeah, Vacco. Vacco, Sacco, Sacco, Vacco . . ." She waved her hand. It's a good thing reporters don't have to face the voters.

This was news I could use. The assistant attorney general for the Criminal Division is in charge of independent prosecutor referrals, which meant my subcommittee's path might soon become considerably easier.

"Emma!" I blurted. "Phil and Romy are coming to D.C., to the Justice Department! Now maybe—" I stopped. Every ear in the room was flapping. "Now maybe we can have some fun and get some work done at the same time! It will be great to get back to working with Phil. He knows everything I know about crime and punishment, and we agree about it all!"

Lanny's eyes rolled. Jerry's eyes rolled. Marian Stultz smiled. Her initial quarry had escaped her, but now, late in the evening, she had scored. This was better than a tidbit of a story, this was a piece of Washington architecture in the making. The part of the architecture that never shows up in the floor plans.

Part Five

M Y FIRST MOVE MONDAY MORNING was to call Phil Vacco at the U.S. attorney's office in Boston. I could tell over the phone he couldn't get the grin off his face. Yes, it was true, but nothing happens 'til it happens in this business, Senate confirmation was required, he hoped he could count on my support.

"Phil, hello? This is me, Terry, we went into the jungle together, remember? Fifteen banks and credit unions, fifteen motions to dismiss for prosecutorial misconduct, we stuffed them all? Of course, I'll be your lead sponsor. Now, how quick can you get down here? We need to talk."

"They made me swear I wouldn't talk any substance, particularly with members of Congress, 'til I get confirmed. . . ."

Jerry Traugott was standing in front of me with a note: "Robert Emmett on line 2." The premier columnist in town.

"Okay, off the record then. You know me, I know you. How about next weekend? It's Silver Cup in Upperburg on Saturday morning, point-to-point horse races, good place for you to meet senators who will vote on the confirmation, not that they'll remember seeing you there. We'll meet you at Dulles, deal?"

"Deal."

I punched the button for line 2 and boomed, "Bobbeee! How's the co-captain of the All-Asshole team this morning? Oh. Sorry." I punched "hold" and glared at Jerry. "Tell that woman an intern picked up the phone, we'll discipline him, and you'll have to find the senator and have him get back to Mr. Emmett, the senator appears to have left the building."

"Sorry. He was on himself before. . . ."

" 'Sokay. Probably we shouldn't have kept him holding."

"Your voice said you were going to get right off."

"It did, I was, I was. Listen, don't worry about it." Jerry smiled and left.

I had been in office four months and I was thirty-five years old and this job was making me a kindly old man already? Whatever having to put on the jolly face all the time makes you. It gets automatic. I didn't like it. I don't want to grow up. It's not natural to extend yourself for every single bucket o' blood that crosses your path, I don't care what anybody says. Sure, maybe Jerry T. was worth it. But not all the other guys.

I reached around and felt the shoulder muscles at the back of my neck. Packed as stiff as a board. What is going on?

I don't have fifty thousand dollars. Yes you do, I've discussed it. I'm glad to hear that.

WE PICKED UP PHIL AND ROMY VACCO at Dulles at 9:30 A.M. on Saturday and were on our way to Upperburg in two minutes. Airports in the country are a delight to me.

I told Phil and Romy it was a pleasure to see them, and for the first time in many moons, this wasn't a fib. Romy is an Eastern European, Gypsy blood, high cheekbones, high energy. She had campaigned ably and strenuously against me when Phil and I were opposing candidates for DA, then titillated the political and journalistic worlds of Boston by giving me a much-photographed kiss at the press conference where we announced I was hiring Phil as a top assistant.

Phil had, quite simply, made my reputation, and it's always good to see your own success incarnate, even if he didn't have any Gypsy blood.

Despite coming from a large and not at all well-to-do Italian family in East Boston, Phil looks as though he stepped from a catalog: today a Pendleton shirt, Filson jacket, light gray cords, suede wing tips. Brown hair trimmed close, pleasant expression, ramrod posture. A classic courtroom prosecutor.

There was a chilly drizzle when we got to Silver Cup, but no one seemed to mind. On the hill overlooking the track, I saw three members of the D.C. Circuit Court of Appeals, including Chief Judge Norbert Tillotson, to whom I gave a wide berth in view of his central role in appointing independent prosecutors. No sense spending the rest of my life answering grand jury questions about what was or was not said in an ex parte conversation with the presiding judge. That's where criminal experience comes in handy: a lot of senators in my position would have barged right up to him, to show they weren't in awe. Would Emma call that chivvying, or display?

Lanny had told me Tillotson would be there because his daughter Josie was riding, but the judge was far from a Silver Cup "type." He stood out in his chesterfield and homburg, had taken refuge under an oak, and was blowing into a Styrofoam cup of coffee so it would throw some heat on his face.

On the same sloping ground, we counted seven members of the United States Senate, including majority leader Vivian and his new deputy whip, Tabor Gunn of Virginia, who had replaced the fallen Fox of Maryland. They were the only two not holding drinks. To judge by the decibel level, they appeared to be also the only two who were sober. Senator Gunn, eyeing the Bloody Marys and bullshots all around him, bore the burden of leadership stoically. He had been the University of Virginia starting quarterback for three seasons, two of them when the Cavaliers broke into the top twenty. He still held himself as though he was standing in the pocket, and might rifle a forty-yard pass at any time. No trajectory, either.

Meanwhile, sign after sign proclaimed that alcohol was strictly forbidden on the premises. I enjoyed the visual dissonance.

The races were spaced at fifteen-minute intervals, so Emma and Romy insisted we traipse through the mud over to the horse stalls, to get a behind-the-scenes peek. I dug an old pair of Rockports out of the detritus in the back of my Blazer and lent them to Phil.

The jockeys, mostly young society women, were chattering and shivering in their silks behind the stalls, while vertical blankets of steam rose from the horses' backs. Too bad the jockeys couldn't wrap up in them. The film director Truffaut, I thought, could do a lot with this.

Emma and Romy chatted with the riders, and they seemed to absorb the energy and perk up a little. We kept slogging around to the main stable, though all the horses racing were now out in the individual stalls.

Phil was walking ahead. As he turned the corner of the stable, he bumped straight into a man coming the other way, knocking off his porkpie hat. The man had been looking over his shoulder. He bent to retrieve his hat from the mud, beating Phil to it and waving off Phil's apologies. He stood up and two volts of surprise went through me. It was Senator Gilliam, red in the face from some exertion. Perhaps from picking up his hat. He seemed unaccountably flustered, disproportionately concerned about the mud on that hat. He stood there brushing with his hand at where the mud had been.

More visual dissonance, more buffoonery. Where is Truffaut? Around the corner at a good clip comes a young blonde woman, just emerged from a quite empty stable, hastening to arrange her silks tight within her jodhpurs.

Gilliam coughed. "Senator, you know Miss Tillotson, the judge's daughter? Senator and Mrs. Mullally of Massachusetts."

"Oh, hi, Senator, hi, Mrs. Mullally, I was just changing for my race, I'm afraid I'm going to be late, do you-all know Daddy? Have you seen him?"

"He's over by the clubhouse all forlorn, and you must rescue him as soon as your race is over," said Emma.

"Ooooh. Poor Dadd-*eee!*" Josie cantered off, flicking her whip in the air. Gilliam plodded on after her without further conversation. Emma and Romy exchanged a look.

■

At Phil Vacco's instance, I had been postponing the pleasure of gossiping about the Justice Department with him, but I now felt a decent interval had passed.

"This is a fairly meteoric rise, my friend," I said as I trudged along next to him.

"Oh, I'm not sure assistant AG is even a better job than U.S. attorney. It's higher on the organizational chart, but it's basically a staff job, whereas in Boston I got to run the show."

"What's the attraction, then?"

"Because the vice president fought like crazy for the right to ask me to do it, and she got it, and she asked me. You don't say no under those circumstances. She was responsible for me being in Justice in the first place. She and you, that is."

"So who's your boss—Simon Buffington, Harry Frobisch, or the veep?"

"My commission is signed by Myron Brinker, who's elected by all the people, so I guess the people are my boss."

"Not bad, not bad, you haven't lost all your moves since you became a big shot and stopped trying cases . . ."

"Candidly, it can't be Buffington, he's too red-hot with this independent prosecutor stuff pending against him. The AG I'm supposed to report to daily on what I'm doing, but my sense is that's more a case of info going from me to him than orders from him to me. And the president has many other fish to fry before he ever gets to my little corner of the world. Presidents don't like being near criminal cases anyway."

"Which leaves the veep."

"Which leaves the veep, which is fine with me." Phil kicked a clotted mud ball at a fence, hoisting it over the second rail.

"Three points, nice shot," I said. If Phil didn't mind that his corduroys and my boots were caked beyond recognition, I didn't either.

"We saw her at the White House. She said she talks to you all the time."

"An amazing but true fact," said Phil, shaking his head in wonder. "I don't think she feels she has many safe harbors, and I'm one of them."

"She's on the level?"

"Straight as anybody I've ever worked with."

"That's good news. So how do they keep house together, her and Frobisch and Buffington? I don't see it."

"I don't see it either. Short-term relationship. I almost think she's got to bolt and run by herself."

So Phil Vacco and Happy Gilliam, who have little in common, not party registration, not degree of rectitude, both foresee a split-up of the Republican ticket. That's got to be worth something, to Marian Stultz or somebody. I decided to change the subject, so as not to look unduly interested.

"How's the office doing? In Boston, I mean."

"Definitely on a roll, fifty-six in a row. Almost makes me nervous. You know what they say, 'The government wishes to win each case, but not every case.'"

"Just let that cleansing loss not be mine."

"Let it not be mine." Phil nodded, laughing.

"What's the diet? The Cosa Nostra guys are washed up, *finito,* right? No more Italian organized crime?"

"Right, now it's Asian OC . . . Asian OC . . . Asian OC . . . as far as the eye can see. Toronto, New York, Wilmington. That's not even including the Pacific Coast."

I felt another shooting pulse, like what you get when you touch a cattle wire.

"Sounds like old home week," I said. Several of the bank fraud cases Vacco and I had handled together involved Asian organized crime figures.

"Not quite. The Ping On in Boston is directing *nada* now. It's all New York. Our office, in fact, has been sort of on the fringes; but I'm about to get the whole ball of wax."

"Meaning, the Criminal Division?"

"Meaning at Crim Div."

I felt the jolt again. Phil Vacco, my good friend Phil Vacco, was going to be in a position to learn a great deal about certain matters in which I retained an abiding interest. Like, the fate of the late Rudy Solano's prize snitch and hired assassin, for example. I thought of Rudy looking me straight in the eye, assuring me, "Doesn't know you exist." Better be true. And now I'm closer to finding out for sure.

Yes, there were a number of historical questions I needed answers to. There was also a problem: they were questions I could not ask, not of Phil Vacco or anyone else.

■

THE ARRIVAL IN TOWN of my straight-arrow prosecutor friend served as a forcible reminder that I had a loose end or two to tie up with Happy Gilliam.

I reached out for him early the next week and was told he was working out of his Texas district office. I called there and was advised he had left for Washington on a noon Sunday flight. Judging it best not to bother Mrs. Gilliam at home with scheduling questions, I again dialed his office in the Hart Building and asked to be put through to his administrative assistant, Julie Bostwick. Gilliam had told me to go through her when I needed something. ("You'll like Julie. She has a good figure and a good personality." In that order.)

"This is Julie."

"Terry Mullally here. You're the senator's AA?"

"Yes, Senator, of course, what can I do for you?"

"I'd like to speak with Senator Gilliam about a matter. Is he around, by any chance?"

"Why, certainly, sir, he's calling in frequently for his messages and I'm in regular touch with him. Is this anything I could perhaps get to work on? I'd be happy to come by your office, sir, or meet you or a staff member outside the building, anywhere, if that's more convenient. Sir."

So that answers that question. Wherever he is, he's in a bungalow. Good staff work, though: when they ask if the boss is available, you say no if the answer is yes and yes if the answer is no.

"Just if you could have him call. Thanks very much, Julie."

"Yes, sir, will do. Thank *you* for remembering my name. I appreciate it."

Wow. Talk about upwardly mobile. I suppose a lot of people, even a lot of senators, go for that big hello. Maybe even particularly senators. It's hard to have your backside kissed all day long without getting your head turned.

I now attended to the delightful stack of personal bills on my desk. Maintaining two pricey residential establishments was something new for this South Brooklyn kid, and we were receiving quite a lot of hysterical rose-colored notices from credit card companies, insurance companies, banks, and upscale retailers. Nothing serious or out of the ordinary, you understand, just a steady stream of commercial hate mail.

I'm trying to consolidate our debts with a single wraparound mortgage, but the problem is nobody knows me as a credit except in Boston, and there I had indicted fifteen financial institutions on my way to the Senate, so they don't exactly roll out the red carpet. I handle the bills by myself. I'm not eager to have this stuff show up on interoffice routing slips. And I don't do it at home because it drives Emma nuts. She's from old money and the money's gone.

I don't have fifty thousand dollars to spare yes you do I'm glad to hear that.

Must speak to Gilliam. Must tie up loose ends.

Again I had a vision of Emma in a hammock, swinging carefree under a blue sky with perfect fleecy white clouds. I felt an ache. What is so bad about having money, anyway? Why do they want you not to have money? What business is it of theirs? We're sent here by the people to vote, not to be poor.

The true danger is corrosion of the system, and I'm tough-minded enough to see that coming a mile away. As long as the system isn't corroded ...

Emma is it for me, you see. My mother died in child-birth—mine. And Emma and I are going to have a hard time having kids, even though we're dying for them. That's what two docs have told us, anyway. That's just how it is.

I have only two pictures of my mother, tiny blurred black-and-whites, can you believe it? And none of my grand-parents.

I put down the hysterical letter from the mortgage com-pany and reached for my billfold to take out the picture of the girl with pretty eyes and braids, in what looks to be a gingham frock. She's looking sort of over her shoulder. At my father, maybe? Her husband-to-be? This is as close to her as I get.

I jumped a mile when the phone went off. This has been happening to me a lot lately.

"Terry Mullally."

"Senator, it's Happy. I can be in your office in an hour and fifteen minutes. Would that suit?"

So, local bungalow, Virginia or Maryland, not Texas. Happy probably can't do Texas bungalows anyway, he's kind of a landmark down there.

"It's a date."

GILLIAM WAS ON TIME, and full of cheer. He closed the door to the inner office nice and tight.

"How can I be of service?"

"Further to our conversation of the other evening, or rather *your* conversation with Ms. Stultz of the fourth es-tate ..."

Happy looked down, musing. "Yes, yes, what a witch. But not a terribly dangerous one. She's almost as slow as she claims to be, to front all that openly. She should have done more homework first."

"That's, I suppose, as it may be. I thought she had done quite a lot of homework, at least more than I would have liked. There remains, however, the matter of my skirts."

"Your what?"

"Skirts. Can't have any dirty mud on the clean little good-government northeastern skirts, can we?"

"Oh, no, of course not, Senator, and, frankly, I thought we had left the matter in perfect equipoise. Just where it should be. Both from the point of view of the, ah, overall situation, and from your point of view personally."

"What is that supposed to mean, I mean, what does that mean?"

"I told you I had had the necessary discussions. You're being taken care of, rather, the matter is being taken care of, but this—it—is no doing of yours."

"I'm being taken care of?"

"That is correct, sir."

"I haven't seen a penny of the, uh, what I discussed with that nice, uh, person, mutual acquaintance of ours."

"I know who you mean. Well, let me ask you, have you completed your review of her, of their, issues?"

Oh! Forgot about that! Gilliam had got this train going along the track ahead of itself, with all his talk. Can't admit we entirely forgot the preliminaries, though, can we.

"I have."

"And?"

"Of course, they're perfectly right on the merits, as I'm sure you know and agree. We have a committee meeting coming up. I can let my position be publicly known there. Better for the public and the press to hear it first. Always better that way. I reached this decision independently, as I do lots of decisions, make decisions every day."

Happy smiled. "As do we all. Status quo on supports would be your view then, no change?"

"If it ain't broke, don't fix it."

I felt a weight in my stomach. I had once fired a man for

excusing his lack of initiative by using those precise words. Not so long ago, either.

"Well, that's good news."

We both sat awhile. Finally, Happy spoke up.

"I would think perhaps half the program might be traditional, half off balance sheet, so to speak."

The program?

"Half and half, eh?"

"Or whatever. Just a thought." He looked dreamily out the window, then at his watch. I had to make a decision whether to make the conversation more specific. Clearly, it would require an affirmative effort to do so. Razor-sharp Happy Gilliam was now the picture of vagueness, lassitude.

Don't ask open-ended questions of a potentially hostile witness unless you know the answer. Never, ever ask a "why" question on cross-examination.

Happy looked up at me, could see I was keeping my powder dry.

"Not to worry, we'll take care of everything," he said, and got up to go. At the door he turned.

"Sometime soon we should discuss the other thing," he said.

This time, I didn't have to ask what he meant. The "other thing" is what senators who want to be president call their presidential campaigns before they're allowed to talk about them.

"Be delighted to, Senator, it will be my pleasure."

I saw a start in his expression. He was reading in more than I had intended.

"To discuss it, to go over it, will be a pleasure," I went on, not quite seamlessly. "I've made no commitment, as you know, and will not do so until we have an opportunity to review the politics of the thing in depth."

"Can't ask more than that," said aw-shucks affable Gilliam, and shook my hand. He held it a moment, and looked straight at me.

"I think we could learn a lot from each other, derive a lot

of benefit," he said. Again, I saw a flash of Emma, the postcard of Emma under the Big Sky.

THAT NIGHT, I told Emma I was tinkering with the notion of supporting Gilliam, down the line, for 2000.

"That's great," she said. "We're here four months, you're about to make the same bonehead mistake for the second time? Stay away, stay away." She patted her forehead. "Bonobo intuition."

"With deepest deference, my dear, your vaunted bonobo intuition is rapidly outrunning its own supply lines, which, being fanciful, are hard to outrun."

I was being supercilious because I was irritated, and I was irritated because I knew I was wrong.

"Yes, dear," Emma said.

I should have known that was the time to cut my losses, but I was still on cruise control. You don't learn until you go off cruise control, until you're fully engaged all the time. It's like learning a language: if it doesn't hurt, you're not really improving your skills.

Part Six

MAJORITY LEADER ANSON VIVIAN, wearing his Judiciary Committee chairman's hat, proved to be quite interested in all those boring judges nominated by President Myron P. Brinker. And those invisible federal prosecutors who preside over secret grand jury operations, and can stab you in the back or the face and leave you for dead and say I'm just the lawyer for the people, it was the people, the grand jury representing the people, who made that decision.

All of official Washington knew that the real decision-maker behind these nominations wasn't Myron Brinker, who couldn't have cared less, but Vice President Martha Holloway, who cared a great deal. She loved the trial court and had bargained for the power to call the shot on district judges and U.S. attorneys when Harry Frobisch, the successful campaign manager, offered her a spot on the ticket. Vice President Al Gore had done much the same with environmental policy and the EPA.

All of official Washington enjoyed the thought of how this must have infuriated Frobisch, who insisted on retaining the call on appellate judges, presumably so they could undo the mischief worked by Holloway's minions below. So, I told Emma, Frobisch has more power over the law, but Holloway has more power over the facts; and given the choice, I'll take the facts every time.

On a sweltering afternoon in July, following a particularly tedious hearing on a nominee for the Middle District of Tennessee who was in way over his head, Vivian and I were sunk deep in two crinkled green leather chairs in the committee chairman's unmarked hideaway office, smoking cigars. A brass ashtray stood between us. My companion was amusing himself by tossing balled-up roll call records into, or rather at, the spittoon by the fireplace.

"What's your cigar there, Leader?" I asked, rolling mine in my fingers.

He took a long puff, blew a perfect ring at the spittoon. "Montecristo Number Two." Another puff, another ring. "My little torpedoes. My only vice, my only luxury. Howbout yours?"

"Partagas."

"Partagas, nice work if you can get it." He tapped his ash vaguely to the left. It fell on the carpet and burned there. He ignored it. "Say, if you don't mind me asking you something, where did you get your money? Or where *do* you get your money?"

I minded a lot.

"Nowhere, I don't have any money. I just enjoy a few of the finer things in life."

"For free? A lot of folks would like to be on that gig. Anyhow, this one's worth the few extra bucks, they've exported the Cuban strains everywhere in the world, even islands right next door, they can't replicate the taste. It's the soil. Same with wine, in France: same grapes, same grape pickers, same grape stompers, a few acres away from the magic vineyard? No soap. Or, no Château d'Yquem. People think trees and plants are powerful? It's the land, the earth, that selects the one sugar maple seedling out of ten thousand."

"Same for the wrappers on cigars," I added. "Shade tobacco. Has to be Connecticut River Valley."

Vivian nodded. "Tragedy, all those new roads around Hartford, used to be beautiful drying barns."

"My state is taking up some of the slack now, growing shade tobacco in the western counties."

"Well aware of that, think it's your best crop, never could stand the taste of cranberries. But it's still the Connecticut River Valley, same soil. Point stands."

It occurred to me that Anson Vivian was not the man to

lose an argument gracefully, once he had committed himself. Not that I was arguing.

Vivian pointed his cigar at the fireplace and frowned. "Special soil, special plants and flowers, special people, don't know state lines." This was not particularly subtle, but I decided I would help him along anyway, to save time.

"Anson, how come you haven't asked me to support you for president? Happy has."

"What did you tell him?"

"I told him I'd have to wait."

Vivian blew a ring at the ceiling. "Guess I reckoned you might say that. I thought to give you room and time to get to know the two of us. You want to chew your tobacco twice on this. Besides, it's not in your personal interest to endorse anybody now, and I never ask anyone to do something that's not in his personal interest. Your near-term future is in the Senate, not the Cabinet, so there's no upside and a big downside to you making an early move. The New Hampshire primary is seven months away. Seven months is forever."

"I appreciate the space. But I don't know . . . I never got back to you in advance of the majority leader vote, and I sure blew that one. Washington's a funny place to have to make decisions in."

"It was Tabor Gunn of Old Virginny who told you next time fold your ballot, by the way. I saw you looking around to see but he was too quick for you. Tabor always was quick getting out of the pocket when he had to. Anyway, you should never make decisions in Washington, D.C. When you're in the District, by definition you're under stress. Shouldn't make decisions under stress. You got something you need to think through, my advice, get out of town."

"That what you do?"

He nodded. "I head for the hills. Lincoln County, West by God Virginia. Soon as the Thursday sessions are over, Vanessa and I drive all night, hand off the wheel every two hours, you get to see a lot of different skies, dawn, predawn, pitch black. You can either blare the radio, fine C & W all the way, except for western Maryland, mostly only Christian stuff on the air in parts there. Or you can go silent. We do both. Seven hours by car to Big Ugly, and I never fail to arrive refreshed."

"People in your town like the name Big Ugly?"

He nodded again. "Wouldn't have any other. Home to Big Ugly Creek, Big Ugly Wildlife Management Area, and, most important of all, the Big Ugly *Trumpet*, preserver of our history and morals. You'll find West Virginia a little different, but it's real, and if you like the outdoors, no trouble fitting in. Folks are basically friendly, not like the District, where everybody's on guard. You and the missus would care to visit, you could even do me a good turn, drive me out after the session Thursday, Vaness will already be there. And a lawyer friend of mine needs a ride out, too."

This was huge. I knew better than to hesitate. "Done, we'd love to. A lawyer without a car?"

Vivian laughed, got up and poured himself another cup of coffee. "It's not a close call," he said as he poured a cup for me. "Paulie Kovalla doesn't even *almost* own a car. Never has."

"What does 'not even almost' mean?"

"You'll see. He's my age and then some, hair gone gray and still down to his shoulders, lives alone on Capitol Hill in an apartment lined with empty brandy bottles. His motto is 'There's always room for Rémy.' But he's a seriously good lawyer, Columbia, made partner at some big New York firm, quit to do poverty law, has argued three cases in the U.S. Supreme Court. Lost them all, but his clients never should have gotten near that court in the first place."

"How do you know him?"

"I was two years behind him at Morgantown, the state university. I've known him all my life. He's a Hatfield, as in the Hatfields and the McCoys, and proud of it. I'm from Lincoln, he's from Logan. I turned over the Lincoln County poverty law center to him when I got elected county judge."

"He's a Hatfield and a high-powered Washington lawyer?"

Vivian put a hand on my shoulder.

"Son, you have some learning to do. The Hatfields are a

great family. Henry Drury Hatfield was elected governor of West Virginia, after the feud simmered down a bit. I'm not saying they didn't shoot women and children, during the feud, because they did, but the ruinous forces weren't those two families. It was the railroads, first, and then the coal companies." He blew out smoke. The real Anson Vivian was now standing over me, not the politician.

"I'm not even sure I hold it against those families that they were passionate. A thirty years' war they kept up, all stemming from the theft of a hog. They'd fight at the drop of a hat, and drop it theirselves. We could stand some more sand like that, in this country."

"Haven't we got enough right here in Washington?"

"Not the same, no nobility. You want to hear the latest Myron Brinker joke from my county?"

"I never tire of Myron Brinker jokes."

"What's the difference between a hillbilly and a son of a bitch?"

"I give up."

"The Ohio River."

"You've hated Myron Brinker a long time?"

"Not him, but I've hated everything Myron Brinker stands for since way before I heard his name."

"What's he stand for?"

"Railroads and coal companies, for openers. He's the natural heir to Mark Hanna, the ultimate regular old Ohio boy, the ultimate reactionary. Hanna was horrified when Teddy Roosevelt got to the White House, thought he was a damn cowboy, but he'd be well pleased if he could see its inhabitant today. Been almost exactly a hundred years."

"And you'd like to turn that clock back?"

"Absolutely. That's why I put up with this foolishness."

"Sounds like it's time to get out of town, wouldn't want to act under stress, would we?"

"You'll like Paulie." Vivian stood up, signaling it was time to get back to committee business. "He's an aficionado of the mechanics of life."

■

As IT TURNED OUT, I did like Paulie, though our intro-
duction was not auspicious.

We were unable to leave Thursday afternoon because,
thanks to the Republicans, the Senate had an evening session to
deal with the obvious question of whether the International
Monetary Fund should pay for condoms in Third World coun-
tries. (The Republicans thought not.) It was arranged, therefore, that Emma would pick me and Vivian up at the crescent
driveway outside Hart at 10:30 P.M.; and Attorney Kovalla
would be waiting for us in the little park at Pennsylvania and
Fifth, S.E., at a quarter to eleven.

The Senate was right on time for once, Emma was right on
time, and Vivian and I by definition were right on time, but
when we got to the vest-pocket park in Seward Square, there
was nothing but three winos flung on the beautiful dark green
benches, laughing at who knows what. Vivian was already
asleep in the back, two minutes from the Capitol. That's a skill
you pick up in campaigns. Emma idled the Blazer as I got out
and peered past the park, to see if our passenger was waiting on
the far sidewalk.

One of the winos got up and startled me by walking
quickly in my direction. I instinctively moved between him and
the car, with its precious cargo. Worse, he shot out his hand. I
looked, in some alarm, but there was no gun, no knife.

"Paulie Kovalla," he said.

"Oh, Attorney Kovalla," said I, pumping his hand and
smiling broad-mindedly. "I've heard so much about you from
Senator Vivian. He's in the car already. Do you need to go . . .
do we need to fetch—"

"No, no luggage. I stopped working at eight and changed
for the road, so I'm all set. I'll just want to pick up my tent and
stuff in the woods outside mud, by then we won't care about
the time. I assume Anson's already gone to the world."

"Outside mud?"

"Mud is my hometown. Mud, West Virginia."

Mud and Big Ugly. We would have a backseatful. I heard Emma stifle a giggle behind me.

Paulie's voice was lustrous, resonant, confident, as though he knew a secret. But there was no pretense about him. I had taken him for a wino because of his shoulder-length white hair and filthy shirt and jeans, but he had courtroom bearing. And ostrich boots that probably set him back a thousand dollars. He turned easily to the two other winos, whose eyes and teeth proclaimed they really were winos.

"Well, then, we'll see ya, Boisfeuillet. Later, Beauregard."

"Later," said one. The other nodded dully. "Seee . . ." he finally managed. His head lolled to one side.

Paulie sprang into the back of the Blazer; Anson Vivian was awake and bolt upright, must have sensed company coming.

"So, Mr. Kovalla," said Emma respectfully. "Tell us about Mud."

"Not much more than a wide place in the road, truthfully, ma'am. But it's home. I was raised with a tick in my navel, in a big ole holler, soil so poor you couldn't raise a ruckus on it. We were so deep in the country, the sun set between our place and Route Twenty-one."

"What's that?"

The majority leader interposed: "One of the three Rs: readin', writin', and Route twenty-one, the road to Cleveland."

The road to Cleveland, one of the three Rs. How that must have galled the young Anson Vivian. He hadn't had to wait for Myron Brinker's presidential campaign before he'd studied up on Ohio. It was right there in his face.

"I gather it's been boom-and-bust in your area, and mainly bust, the railroads and the coal companies won, and the people lost?"

Silence from the back seat for several moments. "That's one way to look at it," said Kovalla, "but having given the matter some thought over the years, I've come to the conclusion that's a superficial analysis."

"So who won?" asked Emma.

Again a pause.

"The mountains won," said Kovalla.

"Hard verdict to appeal," said Emma.

"Hard verdict to appeal." Nothing more from the back seat for quite a while.

WE STOPPED FOR FUEL—corned beef hash and ketchup, that is—at 3:00 A.M. at an all-night truckers' place on Route 64 outside White Sulphur Springs. Vivian stayed in the vehicle to sleep, disclaiming any interest in food. I began to sense a discipline about him. Those birdlike movements might be designed to conserve energy.

Conspiracy is in the air at that hour. Paulie disappeared into the kitchen and emerged in a few minutes with one of the waitpersons, a sweet-looking strawberry blonde in a starched white uniform. Her lashes were batting constantly; she was looking at the floor, craning her neck, twisting her feet. Very young, could even be San Quentin quail, underage.

"Reddy, this is Terry and Emma. This here is Reddy Beltwheel. She's never seen the western part of West Virginia."

Paulie evidently caught the glance that Emma and I exchanged, or else he remembered that U.S. senators are never off duty for scandal purposes, particularly his powerful and slumbering benefactor, because he then and there promised to look in on Reddy on his very next trip west, to discuss the matter further. She took it well, looked as if she thought she'd still had a good outing. She said, "Thank you, anyway, sir." She nodded at us. "And ma'am. And sir." They'd not had much time out back, Paulie must have talked fast.

In the parking lot, we played scissors-rock-paper to see who would get to drive into the dawn. I won. Some people assume men are going to want to show rock, to crush the disorganized scissors. I favor paper.

"Plants have been beating rocks for a long time," I lectured Paulie, who had finished last. "Covered them right after the Ice Age. Moss. Then vines. Then blowdowns."

We got back in the car. I looked in the rear-view mirror. Paulie's eyes were surly. I decided the knife was not yet in far enough.

"The rallying cry of rocks in battle is 'Remember the lichens!' But they never think of it 'til it's too late."

"Shoot, Paulie, that unwed lass was between hay and grass, not even husband-high," said Anson Vivian, who had supposedly been asleep while we were indoors.

Paulie's shoulders slumped. He said "Whatever," waved at his seat belt, mumbled "Live free or die," leaned against the left door so as not to disturb Vivian, and was asleep.

Live Free or Die is the New Hampshire motto. These West Virginians seem to understand New England.

■

BEFORE FIRST LIGHT, A MATCH WAS STRUCK behind me. I breathed deep of the cigarette smoke. It was the same brand as Lanny's. Good atmospherics.

"Take this hairpin right up ahead if you don't mind. I'll get my stuff."

I took the turn, switched to four-wheel drive, and in a half mile arrived at what appeared to be a junkyard. Vivian was sitting up with his eyes open, but somehow appeared to be still asleep. No one spoke. Paulie eased out of the Blazer, did not slam the door—obviously a hunter—and made for a pile of wooden pallets covered by a huge, rotting tarp. He kicked a few pieces of lumber, and in a moment dragged out a rolled canvas eight feet long. This was his tent, also housed his outdoor gear. He fished around and removed a couple of items, then lashed the canvas across the back of the truck, doubling our width. The whole operation took three minutes. Emma and Anson were groggy throughout the proceedings. Paulie had been right: at that point, we didn't care about hurrying to save time.

A half hour out from Big Ugly, it was light enough to see. Vivian was leaning forward between the two captain's seats.

"I love daybust," he said.

We passed a tree with a refrigerator in it, seventy feet off the ground.

"Mining disaster, thirty years ago," said Vivian. "Coal company dam collapsed. Hundred million gallons of water and sludge into the valley, thirty miles an hour, Saturday morning, a hundred women and children killed in their beds. That's all they ever had, was four rooms and a path. Company basically said it was their fault for sleeping late. Nobody ever took that icebox out of the tree."

"Why would they?" said Emma. "Good historical signpost." Vivian gritted his teeth and nodded. We passed an abandoned school bus, tires gone and windows punched out, on which someone had spray-painted JESUS SAVES.

I drove slow, better to enjoy the play of light on the hills and the side of the road. Sycamores and willows are mysterious, spooky at this time of day, birches sullen. Lombardy poplars and softwoods—cedar and hemlock—formed hedgerows halfway up the hills.

"You don't have any upland shooting round here, do you?"

"Naw, shooting and hunting strictly illegal in West Virginia," said Paulie.

"So I've heard. Hey, that's the second Porsche I've seen next to a trailer home. This doesn't strike me as dope dealer country."

"It isn't," said Anson Vivian. "People here take their pleasures when they can get 'em. It's the mine culture: you might not be here tomorrow. When there's a show, an entertainment of any kind, they never sell any tickets 'til the day of."

"Ooh, that sounds like my husband, many moods, one tense: the present."

Vivian shrugged. "Who knows? Maybe you all belong here." We rode in silence for a minute. The road was bordered by terraces chiseled from the shale.

"We're in Logan County now. DeValance"—I thought Vivian said—"is buried in the cemetery right up yonder."

"DeValance who?"

Another pause from the back. Paulie hesitated, then spoke.

"Devil Anse Hatfield. My great-grandfather."

Oh. "How far to your place?" asked Emma quickly.

"First right after Harts," said Anson Vivian. "Twenty minutes."

The Vivians' old farmhouse was at the end of a mile-and-a-half dirt driveway. Corncrib, hog pen, and chicken coop to the right, barn and silo to the left, a more recent single-room structure to the left of that.

Vanessa Vivian was standing on its stoop as we pulled up. Quite a first sight: beaded buckskin jacket, raven hair, chiseled nose, dark eyes suggesting Mesopotamia.

"Law, you like to never got here," she said. "C'mon, c'mon in, and have a dance."

We stepped inside the raised hall. There were indeed a dozen or so people on the dance floor. But not a bit of music.

"Band left at three," explained Vanessa. "We said if they wouldn't play for free, we didn't want 'em. We can still remember the music, though. Look!" A couple no longer young was swing dancing, and I have to say they made it look good.

The ladies at least had manners, shook hands and smiled, *I'm Vanessa, I'm Emma.* Us menfolk were in no mood for niceties, just wanted to savor the moment.

"What's for breakfast?" I asked.

Paulie Kovalla handed me something heavy. "Bellow Nelson, eighteen year old," he said.

"You mountain hoojy, that was bottled in the barn, and you know it!" said Vivian. "That ain't even passing angel teat. Here." He grabbed the bottle. "Hmm, does drink easy, though."

"Listen, you fruitjar-sucking, hay-shaking brier-hopper, that bottle set me back twenty-three dollar and the revenue stamp's still on the neck!"

"So it is," said Vivian reflectively as he took another swig and handed me the bottle.

A few minutes later, I stepped out to enjoy the dawn. Fog rolled like lava down the valley to the west. I walked toward the reddening part of the sky, down a lane framed by honeysuckle, brambles, and Virginia creeper.

Past the first post on the left lay an enormous blown-down oak whose mud-caked roots housed a larval civilization. With a boy's instinct for destruction, I picked up a stick and struck at the side of the roots. Two square feet of matted earth and grass fell away, revealing a cross-section diorama of insects at work. Carpenter ants, maggots, worms, beetles, larvae—future butterflies, future wasps, impossible to tell. Most raced madly across new traffic intersections created by the planar change. Others cringed from the light and air. I would sooner have seen this than the Crystal Palace Exhibition.

After a spell of voyeurism, I walked about forty yards, my hands in my pockets. Something distinctly nonvegetal was buried in the vines on the right. I sauntered over. It was a 1940s farm truck, rusted and overgrown. It had returned to the earth. A Kentucky coffee tree had grown straight up between the high-roofed cab and the flatbed. I stared at the riot of textures and colors in the half-light.

"Air-conditioned model, latest thing," said Anson Vivian's voice behind me. I smelled the Montecristo.

"It's the most beautiful vehicle I've ever seen, I've got to test-drive her, take her for a spin." I pulled away some of the honeysuckle and reached for the cab door.

Anson grabbed my arm, startling me. "I wouldn't do that."

"Why not?"

"Well, one reason is more copperheads live in that truck than in most counties in West by God Virginia, and they think it's *their* truck."

"Is that the only reason? Well, snakes aren't stupid; I say they're *right*." I allowed a measure of space to develop between me and the cab door. Actually, between me and that side of the lane.

Anson fell in beside me, puffing away. The lane eventually dead-ended at an indescribably filthy and disorganized truck garden, fringed with flowers and littered with half-buried coffee cans, porter bottles, unrecognizable and obsolete farm implements, glass jars, and crumpled papers.

"This here is my pride and joy," said Vivian. "Sparrowgrass, rampers, bubbybush, baby tears, laylocks, and sang root. That last is a cash crop, also called blue ginseng."

"Are those tomato plants?"

"They do be love apples, yessir."

Most of the tomatoes were still green, but one plant had fully ripened.

"Okay to have one, to wash down the Bellow Nelson?"

Anson shook his head. "You'll find those ones hollowed out, rotten. A tomato plant races ahead of the season like that when it gets a fungus. It knows it's going to die, so it's desperate to ripen and drop its seeds on the ground. That's how they reproduce. Plant altruism, a beautiful thing, but not to eat."

I squeezed a bulb of unnatural red. It imploded at my touch. Maybe Anson could teach Ruthie a thing or two about plant sex.

"What'll I do if you leave me out here in the country all alone? I'll be dead in a matter of hours."

Anson laughed. "You'll get the hang of it. It's nature's way. Sort of like a hectic flush, when someone's sick. It's easier to understand than Washington, after you get used to the rhythms."

The whole of the garden was fenced with four-foot wire mesh to keep out rabbits and deer. The right corner post carried additional protection in the form of a small, hand-lettered sign: PRIVATE PROPERTY—KEEP OUT.

I turned to Vivian and gestured at the sign. "So this," I said, "is after all where the nation's great decisions are made."

"Congratulations, my son, you have discovered America,

this is that stress-free environment where the decisions are made. Here, have a smoke."

I was impressed. Anson Vivian was a man of parts. I stared openly at him. He didn't mind. He was at home.

The contest for the Democratic nomination in 2000 was going to be a great prizefight between Vivian and Gilliam, and I was going to have a view from inside the ring.

Only problem was, the view would be from both corners.

Part Seven

WHILE I WAS GRATEFUL TO ANSON VIVIAN for the quality time in Big Ugly, I was soon to get into two serious dustups as a result of his saddling me with that investigative subcommittee. My instincts had been right: if I hadn't been the point man on independent prosecutors, they wouldn't have gotten so interested when my name and then my voice came up on the wiretaps.

Two separate wiretaps. And I'm as surveillance-conscious as they come.

On Wednesday, July 14, I got to the office around 8:15 A.M. to review finance prospect lists. I would be going over to the Humphrey Center later that day to make fund-raising calls. Can't do the dialing from government property—everybody knows that—but you have to have your agenda and your substories straight before you arrive at the center, it's like a dental clinic there and you can't think. A lot of the major donors don't care for each other, so you do need substories.

The receptionist said I had just missed two early drop-bys, an Asian gentleman who would not leave a card and a Mr. McKettrick from the timber industry PAC, they understood my environmental concerns but were most interested in speaking with me, he had seemed earnest, a nice young man, well-spoken, fine haircut, had merely asked her to mention to her boss that it's "not a zero-sum game," those were his exact words, she didn't know, of course, but didn't he perhaps have a point? Her expression was entreating. I gave her a blank look.

An Asian gentleman who would not leave a card.

"Thanks so much, Ellie. I appreciate, I do appreciate that.

Here, please let me have Mr. McKettrick's card." She was in heaven. Best tread lightly, not puncture that reverie. I stood in front of her and rubbed the top of my head. Finally, she looked up.

"The, uh, other gentleman, did he say his business?"

"No, he seemed like, almost, not very talkative, you know? Like *secretive,* almost."

"Mmm. Interesting. What did he look like?"

"Oh, coat and tie, he wasn't off the street or anything, I thought he was probably a fund-raiser because he didn't want to talk in the office. I'm sure he'll call, he said he would. Said he was going to Wilmington on business, but would call. Striking-looking man—not my type, Senator, but striking looks." Her eyelashes fluttered. "Large eyebrows."

"Thanks, thanks so much, Helen."

"Ellie."

"Yes, Ellie, of course, I appreciate it." I staggered toward my office door.

"Senator!"

"Yes?"

"You forgot Mr. McKettrick's card."

I accepted the card with an effusive show of gratitude, holding it in both hands and inspecting both sides as I know it is polite to do—no, wait, that's for *Asian* business cards, put this thing in your pocket, you idiot! I closed the door to my office very quietly behind me, not wanting to attract any notice. The creak of the floor as I walked to my desk seemed like a scream. I felt, well, fragile. Didn't feel like talking, okay? Felt like throwing up, in fact.

Large eyebrows. Just what I would have said.

At 11:01 A.M., as not one but two sets of official government logs would reveal, Lanny fielded a long-distance call and buzzed me.

"A gentleman on the line, Boss, Mr. Reed or Ring, has something he would like to share with us, sounds pleased about it. I didn't ask, but I get the sense it may be, uh, dollar-related. He's in a good mood about something. Sounds Asian, which gets my attention both on the minus side and the plus side, where fund-raising is concerned, risk and reward. I asked if he could deal with me instead of being put through to you and he said, 'Yes, of course,' which is why I'm putting him through to you, unless you feel otherwise."

I wasn't likely to feel otherwise. Refer this guy to somebody else, be certain to generate a barrage of follow-up questions from a staffer, in writing, plus alert another human mind to a situation I preferred to wish out of existence.

"Reed? Ring? I don't know him. Major money guys usually don't make cold calls inbound, usually have some meeching intermediary go first." I pretended to reflect for a moment. "But maybe he's major major. Sure, go ahead, put him through."

I punched the blinking button and picked up the phone. "This is Terry Mullally."

"Oh, Senatah Mullally?"

A thousand capsules went off in my head. My skin was tight on my forehead.

"Excuse me?" I said. "Excuse me?" I thought of pretending I could not hear, bad connection, but decided that would only produce a callback. Better to smother this one myself.

"Senatah Mullally, my name is Olie Wing, I am friend of Paul Slifka. And Rudolph Solano. And Christophah Coopah."

I had heard that voice utter three English words, taped by the FBI at the On Leong clubhouse in Brooklyn, New York, in 1993: "I am sure."

I never forgot those words, or that voice, because they were immediately followed, on our Justice Department audiotape and videotape, by a hail of gunfire from Olie Wing's bodyguard, which made hamburger out of the face and chest of two FBI stool pigeons who were attempting to hold up Olie's card game. Olie had fled to Toronto before the FBI could get on the scene to arrest him and everyone else. I had never been able to get the visual of those two violent deaths out of my head: the men were flung against the wall like rag dolls at the same time their human features dissolved into blood.

This was not the type of cognitive dissonance I enjoyed

about Washington. Olie Wing was an Asian organized-crime hit man, and he was calling a United States senator. Last I had heard, Olie Wing was in detention in Hong Kong on suspicion of murder, but he now was in Delaware and had been that morning in my Washington office. I rubbed my forehead at the hairline.

Olie was indeed a "friend" of Paul Slifka and Rudy Solano, two of my closest coworkers in the Police Department when I was in the Brooklyn U.S. attorney's office, but only in the sense that he was a major source of information—and cash—for them. And, eventually, for me. We had given him a break in a case where he could have done hard time, a case where I had been the assistant U.S. attorney on evening duty. Olie apparently never forgot it. But I had never met Olie, and Paul Slifka and Rudy Solano were dead, and the third guy, Cooper, I had never heard of.

Why did I have to have this conversation? Olie was lowlife, a wet boy; I was a United States senator. My transgressions in Brooklyn were long behind me, buried in the sands of time. Yes, they were grains of sand, irritating grains, pearls in oysters, not part of the host. Not part of me.

What would an ordinary person, an ordinary senator, do? How would he act? Inspiration struck. *Treat the caller as a constituent. Routine constituent call.*

"Yes, Mr. Ring, I was of course a good friend of Lieutenant Solano and Officer Slifka years ago, although I am not sure I know the third gentleman you refer to. How can I be helpful? I should advise you that my time is somewhat limited, as I am about to begin a conference call." Not exactly true, but pretty safe.

"Yes, Senatah, I was so sorry hear the death of Officer Solano, he was very good friend, told me so much about you."

Only one option here. "Officer Solano told you about *me?* Whatever about?"

"Oh, many things, many things. He was great admirer of you. Senatah, if it would not be too much trouble, I would appreciate we could have the opportunity to have talk, just little talk."

"Well, Mr. Ring—"

"Name is Wing, Olie Wing."

"Yes—" I omitted any form of address, it would be a lose-lose proposition now, don't want to use the wrong name and be corrected again, certainly don't want to use the right name—"you understand of course my schedule is quite hectic, what with the upcoming recess, perhaps you could give me a number where I could get back with you. Where are you calling from?" Ouch. Dumb question, what's he supposed to say, organized crime clubhouse? Or FBI headquarters?

"What does that matter?"

"Oh, not at all, it's just that if we were to have an opportunity to, in a, in a less hurried atmosphere"—my desk was bare except for the three fund-raising call lists—"then perhaps it would be convenient if I were to call you at some other mutually convenient point." From some other mutually convenient phone. One without U.S. Senate logs.

"I have plenty time, Senatah. I had problem in Hong Kong, but not now. So I call you again." The line went dead.

Act as though this was a mystifying constituent call. I hardly thought there would be video surveillance into the office of a United States senator, but why take any unnecessary chances? I smiled, shook my head in puzzlement, and strode nonchalantly over to my coffee machine to pour my second mug. Except my arms got mixed up: the left arm was going forward when it should have been sliding back, and vice-versa for the right. How did I do this normally when I knew the TV cameras were following me? I sat back down behind my desk, smiled and shook my head again, lifted the phone to ask the receptionist where that call had come in from, then thought better of it and depressed the cradle with the little finger of my left hand. I tapped with my other fingers on the desk next to the base of the phone set, to justify the presence of my left hand so near the forbidden fruit.

Wait, get a grip. You are allowed to make telephone calls, and decide not to make them. No surveillance footage of you making a telephone call is going to prove a damn thing. All senators, all government officials, make scores or hundreds of calls a day.

Just keep your eye on the ball. Just watch what you say. And do.

I felt like a Mayday pilot who sees the ground coming up. No good talking to anybody now, just have to solve the problem. Nobody to talk to anyway.

Time for a little analysis. Olie had called me, he didn't call the feds or the cops. So his goal must not be to bring me down. I've never met him anyway, he probably couldn't croak me, anything Rudy told him would be rank hearsay, not admissible. So it must be money. But I don't have any money *Yes you do.* He'll probably say it's his money, two hundred seventy grand plus interest. He knows Solano and Slifka are dead, so he can't go to the cops. Would he dare go to the feds? Doubtful. He would look like a nice juicy piece of business to them: the Feebs will not have forgotten the violent death of their stool pigeons. And if Olie's in this country legally, I'll be very surprised. All kinds of exposure. He's been around, he knows the worst fleabag dive in Wilmington, Delaware, beats the hell out of having three pissed-off two-hundred-pound baby-sitters in the witness protection program.

I began to feel a little better. Then I remembered it's not either-or in the criminal world: the feds can always make a deal, reel everybody in. *Officer Solano told me so much about you.*

The same possibilities ran through my mind again and again. I was in a fugue state, not getting anywhere. I punched the intercom.

"Say, Ellie, cancel those fund-raising calls at the Humphrey Center, would you? I've got to get to work on some of these issue papers." I noisily opened and shut the large bottom drawers of my desk, looking for files. Both drawers were empty.

■

My STAFF MEMBERS are used to the boss's "many moods," as Emma calls them, and usually keep quiet about whatever they notice. But the next morning at eleven, Lanny and Jerry came to see me. Asked for an appointment, which is in itself unusual. I faced them from behind my desk. I was spending more and more time behind that solid desk, even holding on to it sometimes. They stood there. Lanny swallowed, then spoke.

"Boss, believe me when I tell you we do not want to know what the matter is, but you gotta get out of this building. You have given Caroline the same research assignment twice in two days and then canceled it both times, you yelled at Bull Flannery at the staff meeting, which you never do, you've called Ellie "Helen" about eight times, and people are starting to roll their eyes."

No sense arguing about any of this.

"The majority leader wants us to join him in Big Ugly sometime to talk about 'the other thing,' " I said. "Maybe we should motor on out tomorrow."

Lanny snapped his fingers. "Go for it," he said.

WE PICKED UP PAULIE KOVALLA at the same park, same bench, at 10:00 A.M. on Friday. His hair was slicked down. He was wearing a three-piece suit with no necktie. One of his companions from the other evening was absent, one was present. Paulie handed him a twenty and a ten as he got up to leave.

"Stay away from the Thunderbird and the Gallo, Boisfeuillet," he said.

"Sure enough. Be seeing you," said Boisfeuillet.

"Not if I see you first," said Paulie. Boisfeuillet laughed. His teeth really were a fright, but he had fine eyes and brows. I wondered where in life he had come from.

"Wanted him to have one good bottle, no more," Paulie explained as he climbed into the back.

"We are duded up today," observed Emma.

"Early motion practice. Only had time to tear off my cravat."

Paulie and I shared the driving on the way out. The traffic on both 81 and 64 was terrible, but I wished it could go on forever. I enjoyed every single thing Paulie said. The stupider the better.

Strange how some people just walk right in on you. Paulie's fifteen years older than I am, I had met him only twice, and I already felt as though he were my brother.

"What's your favorite book?" I asked when we had seemingly exhausted every other idiocy.

"*Huckleberry Finn.*"

"Me too," said Emma. "What's your favorite part?"

"Huck and Jim on the river."

"Me too," I said as I squinted at the dark ribbon of road before us.

AT NIGHTFALL, I was hip deep in green slime, a fishing pole in my hand.

"That's enough, or the creek will take you," Paulie advised from the bank behind me.

"But maybe just another few steps would get you close to the really big ones," urged Emma, standing innocently beside him.

"Disregard, disregard, eight-foot drop-off," Anson Vivian countermanded.

"I know," I snarled over my shoulder, glaring at wide-eyed Emma.

"Roll cast to that ripple in the middle, don't even think about a back cast, it took me an hour to tie that Hairy Mary, don't want to lose her. That's it." I looked back to bask in approval. Vivian frowned. "No need to strip in line while it's in the current, only in slack water. There he is, you rolled him!"

The height of the bank allowed Vivian to see into the pool, so I had to take it on faith that a big trout had just missed my fly. Why was Emma giggling? She wanted to see me all the way into that slime, for sure.

"If you hook him upstream of that birch in the water, you got to horse him a little," said Vivian. "He can't get under all those branches."

"He can't?"

"He can very easily, but if he does, we'll never see him or my leader or my Hairy Mary again. So it's recommended against."

A half hour's casting produced two eight-inch trout, which professional pride, a/k/a the presence of my spouse, constrained me to release. Anson and Paulie showed no interest in taking my place, though clearly they knew every inch of the stream.

"What's that part of the creek called?" I asked.

"Durand's Run," said Paulie. "Named for Bobby Durand, my great-great-uncle, was ambushed here by five McCoys while he was trapping, killed three of them, took a bullet in the shoulder, dropped his gun and swam two minutes underwater to get away. The river was high, they couldn't see him. The two survivors, that is. I'm not sure they wanted to, at that point."

It was past nine o'clock when we trudged up the hill to the house. There was some light in the sky but none indoors. "Throw your dungarees on the hood of the car, they'll dry in the morning," Anson advised. I hesitated. Emma knew why.

"Himself doesn't wear undies under jeans, your lordship," she explained, bowing her head. "Apparently it's a guy thing, the feel of that taut, grainy denim—"

"Neither do I," said Anson. "It's okay, it's all in the family, I just don't want to explain to Vanessa why there's a puddle of standing water in her front hall, which she polishes every week. Nekked men are fine with her, in fact encouraged, but sand and water on the floorboards are not."

I complied with instructions, which made for an unprecedented entrance into the house, at least in my meager experience. Vanessa Vivian fortunately had retired. Anson joined her.

Paulie had pitched his tent somewhere outdoors, did not say good night, just walked out the front door, leaving it open.

"It's blacker than Coaly's tail out here," he said with enthusiasm.

Emma and I unpacked a knapsack, I pulled on some corduroys, and we made a nest for ourselves by falling into the living room sofa.

I dreamt I was walking along the lane with the rusting truck. It was night. I could smell the honeysuckle. There was someone walking beside me. It was my father. He was holding me in his arms. I looked away. He said, "They're nobody's people, and they're plenty good enough for me." I was walking. Again a man beside me. I looked at him. He was Anson Vivian.

■

W E AWAKENED TO A THUNDEROUS "SOO-EE, here soo-ee soo-ee, *hey-yee pig!*" I looked out the window. Paulie Kovalla was standing inside the hog pen, wearing an undertaker's coat and a stovepipe hat, broadcasting feed of indescribable squalor. The pigs evidently loved it, and him. It's not easy to tell if a pig is happy, because its tail is already wiggling, but I was sure these hogs were smiling.

Vanessa was on the stairs, stooping to see out the window. "Oh good, he got the slops," she said with relief.

"What's with the hat?"

"This is Paul's annual Sermon to the Swine. Only time he wears that hat. Or the coat. Good thing, too."

"Now, pigs," we heard a low, patient voice intone, "be not slothful." Many grunts of evident agreement. "I do exhort and adjure you, walk upright with thy ruler and master. I said *upright*, Samantha! He threw a piece of slop at a huge albino sow wallowing deep in the trough. She shook with joy.

"That's a good girl. So, walk also humbly, bearing ever in mind that now we eat uncertainly, as through a slimy mud"—all the pigs stopped eating and looked up, I swear—"but on that day, at the gate of the ultimate porcine skypen, shall you meet an endless string of cast-off half-eaten baconmushroomburgers, face-to-face." Paulie stretched both arms in front of him, palms down. This was good enough for the hogs, who fell back to their feed.

Emma hugged me from behind and left her face on my neck. I saw no reason to move.

She whispered, "There are a lot of people—well, individual beings—around here who remind me of you."

"I'll make some eggs," said Vanessa in a loud voice, and disappeared into the back of the house. Emma began twirling knots in the hair on my chest—all I had on was the corduroys. I decided to busy myself about—meaning, hide behind—the current week's edition of the *Trumpet*.

The lead item was certainly a talker: BIG UGLY WOMAN DIES OF SNAKE BITE.

"She was, too, it's kind of funny." Anson had padded downstairs and was reading over my shoulder. "Fanny McLoghlan, rest her soul, truly could not talk a horse out of a burning barn. It's how the Lord made her. She should have taken juice of juniper." A mongrel coonhound was whining at the door. "Shush, Yellow Watch, you miserable in-and-out dog!" Anson hissed, fetching the poor creature a terrific blow with the flat of his hand.

Vanessa returned with a platter of biscuits and scrambled eggs, slathered in butter and rimmed with what appeared to be onions or leeks. My stomach growled territorially. Food fit for hogs is food fit for kings, in my book anyway.

"Have some ramp eggs and catheads. These ramps are fresh, our own, and I've got a couple pounds left over from the Knights of Pythias ramp dinner you can take back with you. Those there are corn dodgers," she said.

Having slurped an egg-ramp-cathead combo and wiped my mouth with my arm, I studied the framed sign by the door.

The original printed version, in block letters, was DOCTORS AGREE—SMOKING KILLS. Someone had crossed out the last words and substituted ON MAKING MONNEY. I decided this was a place of refuge indeed.

"All set to test the waters?" asked Anson.

"We have to be," said a voice from the door. "I strapped both canoes on the truck last night, in the dark. Almost killed myself."

Paulie had changed his raiment and joined us.

"Pauli Girl, I thought you had a big case coming up in Huntington on Monday! Whatever happened to weekend prep sessions?"

Paulie was sheepish. "We decided to file a mountain demurrer," he said. He waved a hand from side to side. "Went away. We just couldn't deny the horses and acknowledge the corn, we would've been murdered. Would have had to take off for the tall timber."

"Well, good for you!" said Anson, restoring his cigar. "Now maybe we can get some *work* done, on the river!"

"What's a mountain demurrer?" Attorney Mullally felt obliged to ask.

"It's when you sneak into the courthouse the day before trial and steal all the papers in the case," explained Anson. "Clerk or register has nothing to work with, no choice but to dismiss everything. Takes a while for the other side to get back to square one. The clerks will only do it to foreigners."

"Live and learn." Paulie was pointing his finger directly at me. This was a command, not an observation.

Emma rallied to my side and took my arm. "We'll try, we'll try," she said. Paulie dropped the Old Testament finger.

After breakfast, we piled into the back of Anson's pickup, which we shared with six fifty-pound bags of fertilizer marked DRIED BLOOD. Vanessa advised me it was not a brand name, just an accurate label. Pre-FDA, even. "Keeps the deer away," she added. The canoes, rigged onto a wooden frame, made quite a noise as Paulie bounced the truck down the dusty road to Big Ugly Creek.

A fine shagbark hickory stood alone at the end of the barn field. There was a wide gash at about eye level, which the tree had done its best to grow over and around.

"What's that wound in the tree?" I asked whoever would listen.

"Porcupine chewed off some bark, twenty years ago," said the majority leader. I asked him how old he had been when he and Vanessa got married.

"He was twenty-one, I was seventeen," said Vanessa. "I loved the sweat of his body and the dust of his feet."

Anson stared dreamily at the birds twitting past us. "Everybody's out today," he said. "Yanks and yellow hammers, Christ birds and rain crows. There goes a dogwood-winter bird."

"That's a scarlet tanager," I said.

"That's what they're called here," said Anson.

"What's a yank?" Emma asked.

"You call it a nuthatch," said Anson. "It's a 'yank' because it wears the Union coat, dark blue."

I again thought of my father, who used to hold me upside down and call me his little nuthatch.

"Henry going to do that field today?" Anson asked Vanessa.

"I couldn't raise him," she said. "He lazybones."

"Henry ain't lazy," said Anson. "He'll go up a mountain to tree a coon or find you a bear without thinkin' about it. He just won't be tole when to do anything. His time is his, he says, and he'll control it, he'll dispose of it, minute by minute."

Emma, squeezed in the corner, turned to stare at me with new eyes. "Are you *sure* you're not from West Virginia?" she asked in a stage whisper. "Maybe there was a mix-up, some confusion at the hospital. . . ."

"I feel at home in Big Ugly," I said. I saw Paulie's head start to turn. "And in Mud."

"You and Samantha," said Paulie. He was pleased I had remembered his hometown.

We put in just below a stone bridge, where the current created a backwater. Anson stationed Vanessa in the bow of the green fiberglass Old Town, Paulie in the stern, Emma on the bottom in the middle. He ordered me into the wicker seat in the front of the tippier red wooden model.

"Steer for the arrow," my Leader directed. "That's the center of the current. And relax, this could be the Middle Keeney on the New River, or Sweet's Falls on the Gauley, so don't feel sorry for yourself. Paddle hard just as we're getting to the rapids, headway makes it easier to steer. It's just like running for president."

Had I heard that correctly? Like a rube, I looked back. Anson Vivian winked at me.

A train of fledgling hooded mergansers scudded to the bank behind their locomotive mother, to get out of our way.

"Watch for that rock! Tomorrow we'll take you to the church service, you can see the snake-handling. That's kind of like running for president, too."

"What's your strategy, just tell the truth, that way you don't have to remember what you said?" I shouted.

"On the contrary, the patchwork of motivations in a national race and the adjustments necessary to accommodate the interests of coalition members require constant prevarication."

Hmm. Anson apparently had thought this thing through.

"What's your timing?" I called over my shoulder. We were approaching a long stretch of shallow rapids, and the current was rushing us.

"I'm not going to be stampeded by Happy Gilliam. It's only July and there's a couple of jobs I want to finish before I start going around braying like a jackass. Pull with your left or we'll be washed up sideways on that log. Also, Happy thinks it's all about money."

"You don't?"

"I sure don't, or I wouldn't live here. The people who were after gold settled on the coast, or went right through Cumberland Gap. I won't take more than a hundred-dollar contribution from anybody for my campaigns, I just don't think it looks right. Happy thinks that's crazy, that's why we let him run the campaign committee. Happy needs lots of other money, too, to keep all his girls. I don't have girls, except Vanessa, and all she wants is to be left alone in the country."

Ouch. Vivian certainly knew how to put the knife in without using too many words.

"Why do you want to do it? Why strain for the brass ring? It has no intrinsic value."

"We're all softwoods, we can't stand shade, we have to be the tallest. Of course, I'm not sure that's good. The tallest trees in the forest don't have any limbs near the ground because they use up all their energy straining for the light. A beech in a field has limbs a three-year-old can reach to climb. May be more of a life. Look, there's a pileated!" He pronounced it "pile-ate-it." Truly a rural person, at least in his self-image.

I turned around, holding athwart to steady myself. "Are you a religious man, Anson?"

"I have a sense of being part of something larger, and not a very big part. Is that an answer?"

"Depends. What's the something bigger?"

"Everything we can see, and a lot we can't. The inner life of insects at all stages. Milk oozing from limestone. Dying thoughts of human beings in Egypt and China, some time ago. Same continuum."

I decided to concentrate on my paddling. My contribution, though, was purely hypothetical. Neither Anson nor Paulie hit a rock or a log all day. Thing of beauty, as Lanny might say. Got to admire it, even if you can't do it.

ON SUNDAY AFTERNOON, Paulie rode back to Washington with the Vivians, so Emma and I had the Blazer to ourselves.

"Did he ask you about 2000? I thought he said he would."

"He brought it up in the canoe, but it was kind of indirect and I couldn't hear too well because of the river."

"I think you should go with him. These are real people."

"I know, I had a great dream about him. Something about him reminds me of my father. But I feel like I already know him. Gilliam is more of a mystery to me. If I go with him, I would be picking up new allies, maybe new moves."

"You have too many dreams and too many daydreams, Terry. The reason Anson reminds you of your father is because he's like *you*. Gilliam isn't mysterious, he's just unsavory. Now would be a good time to shut off that side of you."

I gripped the wheel a little more tightly. This certainly was beautiful land. The red and chestnut oaks were straining for position. White oak was dominant here. There's an ash. There's a persimmon. And goddammit, we've already had this conversation.

"You don't have to go slumming to have romance, Terry."

"I know that, it's only that I like to add value when I enter a new situation, and I have a question as to what I bring to Anson Vivian's table."

"Just bring yourself," said Emma. "That's what the best hostesses always say."

"Maybe," I said.

IT TURNED OUT we were both wrong. The Washington roller coaster soon dumped into my lap two unlooked-for prizes, both of great potential value to Anson Vivian's presidential campaign. How I handled those two situations is the story of my coming-of-age in Washington. In the end, I delivered one of them and held one back, and neither decision had much to do with Anson Vivian. I never would have had the wit to predict that, before I got to the capital.

Part Eight

THE PRESIDENT OF THE UNITED STATES has a way of turning over the earth in your garden, of changing all your summer plans, even if it's the last thing on his mind.

When the White House announced that Myron Brinker would leave Washington on July 20 for a two-week state visit to both Europe *and* Asia, smart money took it as an unofficial declaration of his candidacy for reelection.

Like every other office in Washington, we held a council of war to review the implications of the White House announcement—for us, that is, not for the country.

We met in Lanny's office, as I like to do when mischief is afoot. This is not merely because I associate Lanny with mischief; the French doors from his office give onto a narrow stone balcony from which one can reenter the building via our small conference room, which has an unmarked and unattended exit to the corridor. So the official guest list for meetings *chez* Lanny, once the door closes, can be modified to meet the requirements of nosy reporters.

Lanny's office is a mess. There are the usual framed political posters—DEWEY DEFEATS TRUMAN, FRED HARRIS FOR PRESIDENT, BLUTOWSKI FOR PRESIDENT, ARIZONA LOVES A FIGHTER (John Lindsay, 1972)—but not a one of them is hung, they're all stacked against chairs.

The walls are covered with pushpinned charts, polls, news clips, population density maps, and U.S. demographic data. They change places daily, depending on Lanny's need to access their content without getting up from his chair or turning his head. Once a sheet of paper is five feet from the desk, it loses pushpin protection and falls to the floor. The process is crueler and more Darwinian than the *New York Times* best-seller list, because the choicest spots are nearly always taken by breathless new arrivals. Such is the half-life of political intelligence.

Bull Flannery, my anchor to Boston, was edging his chair into a corner. He pretended it was so he could lean back against the wall, but we knew the real reason was to get as far away as he could from the ashtray on Lanny's desk, which held a dozen of that morning's Gauloises in various stages of decay. Bull had been a beefy Irish cop and then a beefy Irish sports reporter at the *Boston Gazette* for many years. He still looked both parts. As a concession to the ambient temperature in his new hometown, he was dressed in a red-and-blue madras jacket, green madras pants, checked shirt, and tasseled loafers. He looked ridiculous.

Jerry Traugott had some trouble getting the door shut because of the mass of exiled and used-up documents on the floor. She sang, to the tune of the Rolling Stones' *Yesterday's Papers*, "Who wants yesterday's newsclips? / Who wants yesterday's world?"

After a few nanoseconds, she yielded to impulse and kicked enough detritus out of the way so she could slam the door. This raised a white-and-black cloud.

"Hey! Easy!" said Lanny.

"I bet you were a terror with leaf piles on the forest floor when you were a kid," I said.

"At least they disintegrate physically. These only disintegrate informationwise. Anyway, I still am."

"A terror or a kid?" asked Lanny. She answered by keeping her back to him and throwing another eight-and-a-half-by-eleven-inch cloud into the air.

Flannery brought his chair back to earth. "Ain't got all day," he said. "My take is, this trip brings a whole new can of worms to the table." Bull has mangled the English language for a living for so long he's not about to stop now.

"Coony move by old Mr. Potato Nose," said Lanny from behind the desk. In fact, the president did resemble the actor

W. C. Fields. "Don't say anything, make yourself hugely visible, pretty soon everybody figures what is, is right, you must be indispensable. Much better than looking hungry for it."

"I don't think he really enjoys the job anymore," said Jerry. "I mean, I don't think he is hungry for it, or anything else. He just doesn't want to be upstaged by Martha Holloway for his last eighteen months in office, and if he doesn't run, that's exactly what happens."

"Jerry, you used to be such a nice girl. You've not even been in Washington six months. Do you really believe that demonic male ego could be guiding the affairs of our great nation?"

"No, of course not." She laughed and studied the mass of papers on the floor, then looked up. "It wouldn't even be one hundred percent irrational. The veep gave a huge interview to the *Tribune* for this coming Sunday's paper—should be on your wall, Lan, I've seen it in galleys—where she all but said they should appoint an independent prosecutor for Buffington as well as Withers, and just let the chips fall where they may. Marian asked her how that squared with the letters Frobisch has sent to Judiciary, and she said, quote, 'It doesn't.' She's got more testosterone than anybody else in the administration."

"Yes, I can see how the Ohio crowd might take that as vaguely threatening."

"This all says more to Phil Vacco than it does to us," Lanny observed. "It puts him in an interesting situation."

"What do you mean?" asked Bull.

"Ordinarily, you don't buck your patron, especially if your patron is the sitting vice president of the United States. But if you're in a basically military organization, which the Justice Department is, you don't hardly tell your superior you disagree with his order." He crushed a Gauloise stub into the ashtray, to reinforce his point. This meant he wasn't sure of it.

"I don't know," I said. "As between Washington and the field, DOJ is quite decentralized, lots of power in the hands of the U.S. attorneys. All they cared about when I was in Brooklyn was did we spell the attorney general's name right in the press release."

"But this isn't between Washington and the field, this is all within Tenth and Constitution, same elevator bank, even. Phil's going to have to be loyal to his department."

I twisted my head uncomfortably. "Maybe some room for loyalty in politics," I said. "No room for loyalty in law enforcement. Not personal loyalty, anyway. The law can't be a respecter of persons."

Lanny and Jerry laughed at what they thought was a fine piece of sarcasm, but stopped as my face showed otherwise. "So I would trust Phil Vacco to do the right thing," I said. Bull nodded and said, "For sure." This meant he had no idea what I was talking about.

"That's all the Fifth Floor and the department will be asking him to do, at least out loud," said Lanny. " 'Do the right thing!' Wink, wink."

He added, "That's all Sarah Blakeslee is asking *you* to do." I glared at Lanny but quickly saw it would be too much trouble to explain the distinction.

What was the distinction, anyway?

■

EMMA WAS WAITING ON THE FRONT PORCH when I disembarked on Olive Street that evening and scaled my eucalyptus token over the fence. She had on a pink-and-white shirtwaist dress, bare feet, and a big smile. She was hugging her knees.

"I hope you wore more than that to Johns Hopkins today," I said. "Must remember, professionalism above all. Doctorates are serious business. I'd recommend charcoal gray, to the neck and ankle."

She smiled and offered me a delicious kiss as I reached the top of the crumbling stone steps. Shabby genteel, keeps the burglars away. We never lock our house, same reason. (We don't live in Georgetown anymore, or I wouldn't tell this.)

"The White House social secretary called," said Emma.

I assumed she was joking. "Yes, hands across the aisle, doubtless he wants us on the trip, maybe the prez and I can just settle these silly legal questions once and for all, and of course you'll *love* Hortense, you're two peas in a pod . . ."

"It was for the vice president. She has Camp David while Brinker's away, invited us for the weekend of the twenty-fourth. Mostly Republicans, including Phil and Romy, but Happy Gilliam is going, and Judge Tillotson at least for Saturday, so they thought we might 'fit in'—their words, not mine. They said some financial types would be there, too. Maybe they have to have Democrats so it won't look like a fund-raiser, I don't know. I'm dying to go, so I don't really care what their reasons are. Only bad thing is I have to leave Sunday morning for the seminar at Johns Hopkins."

"They told you the Vaccos and Gilliam and Tillotson would be there?"

"Yep. Why?"

"Before or after you said yes?"

"Oh, I know better than that. I said I'd have to ask you. But I was pretty friendly."

"No harm in that," I said. This was a poser. Vacco, Gilliam, and Tillotson: pretty much ringed my official responsibilities, both on offense and defense. Phil represented my past exposure, Gilliam was my current exposure—two shots across my bow? And Chief Judge Tillotson, I was pretty sure, was where the veep would like me to steer the independent prosecutor cases. So that was something I could do for her. Maybe just coincidence.

"The person who called, was it a secretary, protocol office, that sort of thing?"

"No, but she was very nice. Said her name was Tara Johnson or Johnston, the vice—"

"The vice president's chief of staff."

"Right. Good guess! Now, can we go?"

• • •

THE VISIBILITY WAS POOR on Saturday morning as the Blazer ascended the winding slope to the wrought-iron gate with mounted TV surveillance cameras.

"Are these the foothills?" asked Emma. "Do we get to go up high from here?"

"We stand virtually at the summit of the glorious and storied Catoctin *Mountains,*" I said. "Though I warrant you they would be called hills or bumps in any other state—excepting perhaps Massachusetts. So, what say we go along with the gag."

"That's my motto for the weekend, go along and get along."

"You're in the right place for it. There's about a trillion dollars represented at the cocktail party tonight, according to the list."

The guards at the gate weren't fooling around, and didn't seem impressed with my rank. We had to pull over to a slab on the edge of the hill and open the rear hatch of the truck, whereupon a suspicious German shepherd all but crawled up into Emma's canvas jacket on the floor. We were waved through after a full two minutes, by unsmiling figures.

"*That* was fun," said Emma. "What do they think, we're all going to sit around and smoke dope with the vice president?"

"That dog couldn't smell ten keys of hash if you mixed it in with the Alpo. That was explosives all the way, semtech, plastics."

"So the fat old guy in *The Graduate* is right when he says, 'I've got one word for you, son: plastics'?"

"I might give that joke a pass this evening if there are guys with dangling earpieces hanging around your circle."

The standing timber, as we continued up the driveway, was fourth growth at best. Only the mist gave the view some drama.

"I'm glad it's foggy," said Emma. "Makes it seem more like a mountaintop, more like Shangri-la." She hesitated. "I hope it doesn't mean we'll be two hundred years old when we go back down into the valley, like the lady in *Lost Horizon*."

We crunched to a stop outside a cabin marked "Laurel." Phil Vacco opened the driver's door while I was still folding the map of Maryland.

"Welcome to Camp David," he said agreeably. "One way how to know when you've arrived."

"Right, the car stops," I muttered.

"You big phony," said Emma, poking me in the ribs. "You know you can't wait to start hobnobbing with that glamorous vice president and all those zillionaires. Even if the trees are too thin and the cabins are painted madhouse green."

Emma had to admit that our cabin was tastefully appointed inside: large bedrooms impeccably furnished in cherry, cedar, and teak, each with its own bath and dressing area, and a comfortable common room dominated by a huge stone fireplace, roaring already at this hour. Decades' worth of *Gray's Sporting Journal* filled the bookshelves and coffee tables, and an assemblage of bamboo rods and trout flies put me in mind that Herbert Hoover had used this place as a fishing retreat well before FDR christened it "Shangri-la."

"Let's go for a walk, I have to show you something," said Phil quietly, before we could settle in front of the fire.

"Oh, good," cried Romy, clapping her hands, but Phil turned to give her a look and her head sank.

"Uh-oh, looks like more boytalk yet once again," said Emma. "C'mon, Rome, we'll go out first and throw a Frisbee, get soaking wet, and get the first baths." Emma had seen the lion's-paw tubs, a favorite of hers.

Romy seemed unconvinced this was a good plan; Emma virtually dragged her out the door. To exclude Romy from anything was uncharacteristic of Phil Vacco, so I knew something was up. I figured I would just wait, and it would come clear. Which it did—eventually.

■

PHIL AND I PUT ON TWO of the air force parkas that hung behind the front door, shoved our hands in our pockets, and pretended we were P-38 pilots as we strolled toward the tennis courts and helipad. At least, that's what I was doing. When we were most of the way there, Phil hooked right down a paved lane that led to a squat wooden structure.

"Looks like a German pillbox," I said.

"More than you know," said Phil.

We ducked and went in. Two polite young marines, one male and one female, thrust automatic machine guns into our hands.

"Good morning, Mr. Assistant Attorney General, good morning, Senator Mullally, glad to have you visit us, here are your weapons, sir, and there are the screens." So, I thought, maybe they don't put the A team at the guardhouse on the road, maybe this is the A team.

"Have you done the simulated firing before, Senator?" I looked at the two movie screens on the wall, at a loss. The marine didn't need to wait for an answer.

"We will darken the room, sir, and on your screen will appear a scene exactly as it might appear to a duty officer. The first is the approach to the entrance gate, where you came through. The second is a group of urban terrorists holed up in abandoned buildings. The third is a scene in a bar or nightclub, routine check, routine stop. You may fire whenever you like and as often as you like, the computer will record each of your shots as a red dot on the screen, and keep a running tally of your total score at the conclusion of the video clips: three points for a hit, minus one for a miss, minus five for a bad shooting. You need squeeze the trigger only once, the weapons are fully automatic. Don't worry, they're not shooting anything but air, they're connected to the computer."

She hit a switch, the room went dark, and both screens lit

up with a view of the approach road from the vantage point of the guardhouse. Probably taken from those TV monitors on top of the gate. An American luxury car rolled slowly up the road toward the guardhouse. The unassuming and friendly driver, no mustache, no turban, leaned out the window, smiled, and held out two sets of diplomatic credentials. I looked on with interest, and must have let the point of my gun sink toward the floor.

When the car was ten feet from the gate, the driver jerked his head and arm back into the car, hit the floor, and accelerated into the gate. Something came out of the sunroof of the car and there was an explosion just to my right. At the same time, both back doors were flung open and four men in commando gear, two on each side, rolled out onto the ground and began firing toward my position. I was deader than a dead duck before I had the machine gun halfway up to my waist. The computer knew this, and would not let me register any red X's on the screen.

"Okay, on to the next one," said the kindly marine. I glanced over and saw that Phil Vacco had killed three of the terrorists; they were covered with red X's and were frozen motionless on his screen.

The second scene was an urban wasteland. The camera was advancing, with a somewhat jerky motion—handheld, evidently—on a burned-out building with lots of tall, thin windows. I kept the machine gun at eye level and resolved that I would not be offed again, at least not so easily. A hooded figure appeared briefly at an upstairs window. I dinged him right on his breastplate. "Nice shot, Senator," said the corporal. Another figure appeared in the downstairs doorway; almost in the same motion I swung down and covered it with red X's. Even through the X's, though, I could see the letters "ATF" emblazoned across his back.

"Afraid that was a mistake, sir," said the female marine. "That was one of ours, sent in to to secure the ground floor." I groaned. Phil laughed. "Guy has more lives than a cat," he said. "I popped him off early this morning, but not quite so good as you did."

The third video was an interminable walk up a lushly carpeted hotel hallway, past many potted palms and hanging spider plants, through a restaurant area to a bar/lounge filled with jolly people in Hawaiian shirts, holding tropical drinks. I was a little jumpy at first—almost shot a chandelier by mistake—but soon fell into the carnival mood, figuring this was a "control" designed to stampede you into blowing away a family of Japanese tourists.

A burly man with a blond flattop haircut, wearing a flowered shirt and blue shorts, seemed to be arguing with two women at a marble bar area along a wall to the side. They were seated on stools with their backs to us. You could see their faces in the mirror, though not their hands and drinks. The camera stopped fifteen feet from them: the duty officer must be saying something. The man turned around and got off his stool, quite angry, but did not advance toward the camera. He wasn't angry at us, apparently, only his female friends. The woman in the center pivoted on her stool, and in the confusion dropped her drink onto the floor, where my eyes followed it. I noticed she had on high heels. I heard the click signifying that my gun had jammed again, and looked up to see that the other woman had turned around on her stool and fired a pistol from waist level directly at the camera.

"Based on a real-life incident," said the male marine grudgingly. "Enna Morash, top drug smuggler. In real life, the officer survived, barely, but in here she gets him every time."

I was checking my body for bullet holes as we emerged into the daylight. "I feel like Swiss cheese," I said. "Was that what you had to tell me, that I have lousy reflexes and I'm a lousy shot, so it's amazing I've ever killed a deer?"

Vacco smiled. "That was just the warm-up," he said. He picked up a stone and sailed it over the lip of the hill.

"Remember I told you we have been playing at the edges of Asian OC in the Boston office, and I was looking forward to getting my hands on the whole enchilada?"

"Yeah, maybe more properly the whole spring roll."

"Well, I have, and the department has turned a whole

bunch of guys, mostly in New York and San Francisco, a couple in Toronto, and some in Hong Kong. The picture that emerges is not a pretty one, which won't surprise you. It's like the mob during Prohibition, or La Cosa Nostra in the old days, they've corrupted the so-called good guys at just about every level."

"Tell me something I don't already know."

Phil stopped and squared to face me.

"I'm going to tell you something you don't know. We have three independent sources who say that the late Rudy Solano, your pal, was on the pad and bagging cases throughout his career. We don't think it can be a coincidence: one witness Toronto, one New York, and one Hong Kong. The guy in Hong Kong is in Technicolor. Bad boy, wet boy. I shouldn't even be telling you this, but I know how the world works.

"Right now I'm the only guy at the Criminal Division who is aware how closely you worked with Rudy, or at least that you were deer-hunting buddies, too. I'd hate for you to get blindsided on all this by reading about it for the first time in the newspapers. I have not passed the information on to the Fifth Floor, partly because they haven't asked me a direct question, and also I know damn well what they would do with it, given the state of relations between your subcommittee and the White House. I've actually got a guy on my payroll seconded to me by the White House, member in very good standing of the Alexander Hamilton Society, which is Harry Frobisch's ideological petting zoo. I know damn well one of his jobs is to look out for stuff just like this, and run back to 1600 Pennsylvania if he sees it.

"So, if you have any bright ideas as to how to handle this, let's have them."

I looked at Phil Vacco. I picked up a stick and broke it, threw half and let the other half drop.

No sense stirring up the leaves at the bottom of the lake if we don't have to.

"Phil, I am just amazed. I knew Rudy Solano quite well in New York, as you know, for a number of years, even if it was largely social, or rather outdoor pursuits, and I would never in a million years have thought—"

"I know, I know. When you know a guy as a fishing buddy, or hunting, it's not easy to project what he would do in a completely different context. But you worked with him, too. There are lots of records. Somewhere." He looked off to the side.

"Well, yes, it's not as though I was unfamiliar with Rudy's work at the Police Department in New York, he had quite a reputation. He pushed hard, made a lot of cases, and I always thought he was one of the very best, not a bad apple."

"Yeah. Well. Just so you know."

"I appreciate it more than I can say, my friend. You are absolutely right about the misuse that political figures would make of fragmentary information here. Keep me posted, to the extent you can." I zipped my P-38 jacket to the top, then realized this was a ridiculous gesture.

"To the extent I can, I will."

Oh, great. *I* was supposed to refer to the duty of secrecy, not you. *You* were supposed to pooh-pooh it.

My head was swimming again. I was the Dutch boy plugging the holes in the dike with his fingers. Ten fingers, twelve holes. I hate it when that happens.

The next question was even more unsettling. The next question made me forget all about the Dutch boy.

■

Anything else I should know, Terry?" Phil had stopped flinging stones, had his arms folded.

I didn't care for the open-ended nature of the inquiry. Sounds like a perjury trap. Anyone with nothing to hide would be irritated by that question. So, let some irritation show.

"Not that I distinctly recall, at this present point in time. Anything else *I* should know?"

"Actually, there is."

We stopped walking. Both of us squinted off to the side, into the misty woods.

"Oh?" I said casually.

"Part of our renewed emphasis on white-collar stuff, we're looking at securities and commodities pools, market manipulation under Section Nine of the 1934 act, the Securities Exchange Act. Your name has come up in certain conversations to which we're privy. You have any knowledge, anything that could help us?"

Conversations to which we are privy. My mind went into overdrive. Could be an undercover agent, could be a wire. Could be they turned Happy Gilliam. Or Sarah Blakeslee. *Yes you do I've discussed it with Sarah Blakeslee's people.* But the only person I've talked to is Gilliam. Gilliam is the problem. Must assume Gilliam is unreliable.

Instantly I knew I had to choose between dummying up entirely or putting the knife in Gilliam. But it couldn't be too big a knife, or it might cut me. Or get blood on me. How much did the Feds know about Happy? And what had Happy done, anyway?

I had a flash of John Dean telling Nixon during Watergate, "Sir, there's a cancer around your presidency."

Time for Dr. Mullally to operate. Must sever connection. Triage time.

"It rings a faint bell, to tell you the absolute truth. Yes, let me see: it was, I think it was, Happy Gilliam." I pondered, as though dredging up details.

"Yeah, Happy had a couple of bourbons at our house a month or two ago, he and the missus were there, and Emma and some friends of hers and a reporter—we're continuing our old Boston strategy of feeding the beast, you know." I smiled at Phil.

He looked back at me without a smile.

That's it. Got to let Happy have it, pretty much right be-tween the eyes.

"And Happy started, like, almost raving—I told you he'd had a couple of drinks, I distinctly remember him reaching for the Angostura bitters—"

I regretted this immediately. Phil and I had more than once discussed the tendency of professional con men to sprin-kle their "debriefing" stories with what we call "winning and homely details"—very specific assertions, either true or impos-sible to disprove, designed to impress the prosecutor or the FBI agent with the declarant's good faith. We both had radar for these babies, and hated them, would walk out of the room. I elected not to look at Phil again.

"Anyhow," I went on briskly as though snapping out of a dreamy reminiscence, "Happy was burbling on before dinner, something about investments or pools. I was the designated cook, and I had seven dishes bubbling, so I wasn't paying that much attention, but I'm pretty sure that's what it was about," I concluded earnestly, helpfully. I looked at Phil.

I could see I hadn't told him anything he didn't know. So old Happy was on their screen. Thank God I hadn't committed to him for the "other thing": that was going to be two thousand miles of bad road.

For Happy. Not for me. I would make sure of that.

"Thanks very much, Terry," said Phil. "That's very helpful."

If it's helpful to you, I thought, it's going to be even more helpful to Anson Vivian.

But I can't tell Vivian about this, at least not now. I'll have to say something ambiguous to him, something I can refer back to later.

Thank goodness I had time to jump before the train came through. It never hurts when you're friendly with the prose-cutor.

I began to whistle a tune as we resumed our walk back to Laurel. Too late, I realized it was "I wish I was in Dixie," but I finished it, didn't stop or hesitate. That would only have drawn attention.

At the door, I said, "Thanks for the shooting lesson, my friend. Next time I'll do better."

"You didn't do so bad," said Phil. "You shot around five hundred."

There was something in his tone I didn't care for, but I nodded and said, "Right you are!"

■

STEAM WAS ISSUING FROM THE BATHROOM when I let myself into our suite at Laurel Cabin. Upon investigation, I discovered my wife sitting upright in the enormous bathtub, covered from neck down, more or less, with bubble bath. Two scoops of meringue glacé.

Sometimes you just don't have any choice. I kicked off my boots and jeans and settled into the tub behind Emma, bracketing her with my legs.

"I've been wanting to get my hands on these guys," I said.

"You're in quite the hurry. You don't mind your wonderful western shirt is getting wet?"

"No, I don't mind that my wonderful shirt is getting wet."

"Keep doing that."

I closed my eyes and listened to the water draining out. "Is that a gurgle or a gargle?" I asked.

"Never mind, just keep doing that."

I pressed the side of my head against the back of Emma's neck and rocked her forward.

"My arms and hands are very full," I said.

"Apparently that's not all," said Emma. She eased herself up, then down.

"Degree of difficulty, eight or nine? You be the judge," she said.

I pulled her in tighter, then shuddered and lay back against the tub. "It's academic," I said.

"You moronic male, you were too quick," she said. "Now we have to have supplementary proceedings."

On this occasion, I didn't resent my wife's legal training.

DESPITE ALL, THE MULLALLYS AND THE VACCOS presented themselves punctually for the cocktail hour, not to miss anything. Emma was wearing blue satin, and a choker with a fake garnet.

Cocktails at Camp David are served in the living room of the main lodge. Even at the White House, I have never seen such Americana, so many Remingtons and Churches per square inch. The tables and sideboards are littered with derringers, pistols, miniature replicas of ships, boxes of old coins, woodcuts, hand-carved duck and snipe decoys, you name it. Conspicuously absent is any sign advising against handling the merchandise. It is a sportsman's and an antiquarian's paradise. Nothing is behind glass. I guess not too many light-fingered guests make it to Camp David.

The first person we saw when we entered the room was Senator Gilliam, standing by himself with his back to the bar and holding a long glass. As luck would have it, Judge Tillotson and his daughter came in the side door near him. Josie ordered a Virgin Mary, looked in Gilliam's face and said, "Oh, hi, Senator."

"Good to see you," said Gilliam, moving away from the Tillotsons toward us and extending his arm to another arrival.

"Sam, my boy, dee-lighted to see you. You know Senator Mullally, of course, and this is Mr. Philip Vacco, the new head of the Criminal Division at the Justice Department, so anything you say can be used against you, ha, ha . . . Sam Burriss, represents food and milk and all that's wholesome, one of the great ones. A pillar of the estab—, of the people's government."

The new arrival was expensively dressed. Blue blazer, four

brass buttons on each sleeve, silk foulard in his breast pocket. He had slicked-back, thinning sandy hair, freckles, large eyes hollowed out and decadent, a face the ghastly pallor of paper. His dentures formed a death's head rictus seemingly pasted to his chin. He pressed my hand in both of his—they were pudgy and humid—and spoke in a low voice, ready to please:

"Senator, I am *proud* to meet you, I have heard so much about you." He turned to Emma. "And this must be the famous Emma Gallaudette Mullally, formerly of Rankin and Shaw and now of Johns Hopkins fame?" Emma started. Someone had done his homework.

Burriss turned back to me. "Seriously, Senator, many of us were most impressed with your thoughtful speech at the committee meeting the other day, opposing the ill-considered move to undermine long-standing public support for vital commodities."

"Not at all, I simply made a study of the issue, and that's where I came out." I turned my shoulder to try to cut Phil Vacco out of this unwelcome conversation.

"Well, the people I represent particularly appreciated having that conclusion reached by a distinguished member of the committee who does not have a dog in the fight, so to speak. An honest broker, if you will."

I backed up a step. I had heard that argument before, and Burriss, drawing closer to me, reminded me of where.

"I believe you may have met a colleague of mine recently, Sarah Blakeslee?"

"Oh yes, the agribus—, the agriculture lady. Does she work for you?"

Burriss lowered his eyes. "Well, we work together," he said quietly. What a phony.

His head darted up in an entirely different direction, far from our group. "Mr. *Secretary!*" he exclaimed with joy, and trotted toward a huge red-faced man making for the bar. Burriss fell in step with him rather than retard his advance. "I am so *honored* to see you here, sir," he began. At that point, his voice dropped and I heard nothing further of their conversation, though hearing the words would have been superfluous. This guy was all ooze.

At dinner, the secretary of the treasury was seated at the vice president's right, and Assistant Attorney General Vacco—young Phil Vacco, whom I had raised from a pup, who used to work for me—was seated to her left. To his left was my very own bride. I was right behind them at a quiet table filled with dumpy, stoop-shouldered lobbyists, plus Judge Tillotson and Josie. I kept my ears on Emma's circle.

The vice president leaned past Phil Vacco to Emma. "You look like a ruby-throated hummingbird, my dear. But none of the men here have dressed all in red, to attract your attention."

"Men are so stupid," Emma agreed.

"I saw in my briefing book you study both plants and primates. Is that a common combination?"

"The more usual course would be paleoanthropology, then apes, then living foragers. But I like mixing in ethnobotany, to further put us humans in our place."

"I completely agree," said Holloway. "We haven't got much on trees. They feed birds and animals, birds and animals feed us, we're only two steps ahead of trees in the food chain.

"Plus," she went on, waving a finger in the air, "they're as human as we are, anyway. You know the mangrove, that lives on the edge of saltwater? It's kind of the sacred tree of Florida, my state. If its roots soak up too much salt from the bay or the bayou, they send all the excess into one leaf, which turns yellow and falls off. Triage. Saves the tree."

"And trees are so *magnificent!*" cried Emma, happy with this turn.

"Plants are patient, too, unlike humans," said the vice president. "The agave, the century plant, will live for decades without flowering, then one spring it grows a floral stalk the size of a telephone pole, bushy yellow shoots, lots of seeds, and promptly dies."

She popped an upside-down forkful of spinach crêpe into

her mouth. "Give me a live oak or a willow to sit by, and I'll never be bored," she said, tossing in the second half of the crêpe by hand. "Because you get to watch the insects and birds, too. But primates I don't know. What do you get from primates?"

"My best sense is you can get a lot of stuff that's wrong if you don't quantify your data," said Emma, "especially if you're a paranoid male researcher who wants to prove that all hominids and humans are would-be big-game hunters, meat-eaters only."

"I hate that. Happy to hear it's wrong."

"Hominids rarely got big game. As Scotty MacNeish says, they probably got one in a lifetime and never stopped talking about it. He's a great archaeologist. Lizards, starchy pods, pith from palms, arrowroot, clams, larvae—that's what they ate most."

"What about chasing the mastodon, and all that?" asked Phil.

"It's just a theory of the male researchers, that we didn't become hominids 'til our ancestors moved out of the rain forest into the savannah, the open, where they could run down big game. But the more recent evidence, from the pollen record and animal bones, is that hominids probably caused the savannah, not vice versa. Hominids' first cutting tools—Acheulean tools, they're called—coincide with the first evidence of small clearings in the forest. The earliest cultures—the Oldowan—are still in the rain forest."

Martha Holloway had stopped eating and was clearly oblivious to everyone in the room but Emma. "Tell me more," she said. I suppose at her level, you don't get an interesting new information "fix" too often.

"Well, the other thing I wonder about is the 'selfish gene' theory: that individuals select mates and reproduce mainly to maximize the number of their own offspring. Before DNA testing, the postulate was that males would take care only of their own offspring. So the silverback gorilla was conceived of as the head of a harem."

"And after?"

"DNA showed that the majority of the offspring that male birds and animals took care of were not theirs."

"Whew."

"So consortship, the animal version of marriage, is much more a social, not merely a functional, setup. The females prefer the younger males to copulate with, but they spend more of their time with their consorts, the older gorillas and chimps, the alpha males."

"Are there alpha females?" asked Phil.

"Sure. The bonobos, cousins of the chimps, are run by alpha females. They're my particular interest," said Emma. "Everything is more relaxed. Instead of bashing each other, bonobos resolve tension and competition through nonprocreative sex, a kind of petting."

"Sounds like a good model," said the veep. She knew she had to break off now and turned with visible effort to the red-faced man on her right. She patted his arm. "How's Millie doing?" she began.

My attention drifted back to my table and I realized that Sam Burriss was talking. He was explaining that in addition to representing agricultural interests generally, he was also the president of the Committee to Preserve the Everglades Through Sustainable Growth.

"Oh, are you from Florida?" I offered as my first contribution to the success of our table as a group.

He nodded. "Originally, yes." He studied his soup. "I have known the vice president a long time, since her daddy was a judge in the Arcadia courthouse, and while we have not always agreed on every topic, she is a mighty fine lady."

"Wasn't a ban on cutting in the Everglades a big issue in her campaign for governor?" I asked.

Burriss was subdued. He rolled a silver knife between his thumb and forefinger, studying the play of the light. "It was an issue, not one where we were together, and one which got blown out of proportion, I feel, by the national media." What did *this* mean?

Mercifully, we were interrupted by a clumsy waiter. Or perhaps a very astute one: if you are going to find common ground between environmentalists and sugarcane interests, you had better pack a big lunch. Or eat a big dinner.

I turned to Josie Tillotson. "Is this a first for you? It is for us."

"I was here once when Daddy was in Congress, when they really needed him for something," she said, "but I barely remember it." Judge Tillotson frowned.

"Sorry, Pops, I didn't say how you *voted*, after all."

His face lit up as he appreciated his daughter's joke. "I'm just in a foul mood because I have to go back after dinner and give the breakfast speech at the Federal Circuit conference tomorrow," he said. He turned to me. "Don't worry, I won't talk about independent prosecutors!"

I smiled at this: it's almost always best to get into the open what's on everybody's mind, even if only with a glancing reference. Helps everybody relax.

"Don't get me started on *that*," said Sam Burriss.

"I won't, I promise," said Judge Tillotson. This meant, shut up and change the subject, which Burriss understood and did.

The closing prayer was offered by a Baptist minister. The vice president began to drum her fingers on the table as he waxed on about family values, staring directly at her. Burriss saw what I saw, and leaned over to whisper an explanation: "Myron Brinker signed up Reverend Thistle here for the weekend before he knew he was going to be on the trip." I nodded sagely, not daring to risk a smile. Give one point to Burriss, anyway: he can size up a situation.

Martha Holloway gave quite a funny toast at the end of dinner about how this really was a bipartisan affair because she knew damn well all the businesspeople in attendance gave just as much to the Democrats as they did to the Republicans, which was true. She mingled briefly with her guests in the living room—I heard her say "after lunch, not during it" quite firmly to Sam Burriss—and left with two Secret Servicewomen at nine o'clock sharp. That cleared the place out fast, must be protocol.

The Mullallys and the Vaccos read by the fire in Laurel for an hour and a half. Phil seemed out of sorts, didn't want to talk about anything. He wasn't so moody in the Boston office, I thought.

∎

I WOKE AT 5:30 A.M. TO THE COMFORTING SOUND of rain on the roof, eased out of bed, and slipped on my jogging clothes. The path in the woods paralleled the pavement. I was able to make fairly good time for a mile or so, and was thinking how surprising it was there were no Secret Service in sight, when I looked up and saw a video camera on a tree just in front of me. I waved to show I was friendly. Never know when they might have to train some of those very young marines with live rounds.

I doubled around and with a minimum of pavement was able to circumnavigate most of the grounds, returning past the helipad and the main lodge, down the hill toward the guest cabins. I was fighting the rain now, squinting to keep the path in view. I transferred from dirt path to paved walk, as I knew I would have to do for the last few hundred yards. There was an open door with a light behind it. I looked over, what was I supposed to do?, and wished I hadn't. Josie Tillotson was in a white nightgown, her hair loosed, a Raggedy Ann on tiptoes, her arms around the neck of a figure dressed for departure, a figure in a hat. A porkpie hat.

Gilliam removed any doubt as to the character of the kiss by looking furtively behind him. He had executed almost a full sweep before he saw me, in motion, thirty feet away.

There was nothing to do but look straight ahead and run on by.

After ten or fifteen strides, at a curve in the path, I became aware of an animate presence among the trees. Animate but

still: a figure in a raincoat, not moving. It was one of Vice President Holloway's Secret Servicewomen. I was startled to see
her, and she did not seem happy to be seen.

"Good morning, ma'am," I puffed. She nodded but did
not return my greeting.

I looked behind me and saw that the entrance to the
Tillotson cabin was around the bend, not quite visible.

Which meant that the Secret Servicewoman was not quite
visible from the cabin.

BACK AT LAUREL, too, the front door was open and there was
a woman looking out.

It was Emma, staring at the curtain of rain. "You are in the
nick of time," she said. "We want our hairs to look their best for
their important conference." She tossed me the keys to the
Blazer. I caught them without breaking stride and chugged off
to the parking lot.

When I pulled the vehicle up and jumped out, Emma
threw her bag and herself in the passenger side and scooted
over. I gave her a kiss through the driver's window—or tried to,
it turned into an air kiss—and to get revenge began to shake my
head like a Newfoundland puppy.

"Get away from me, you big stupid repulsive dog," she
protested, pushing my head out the window with the very tips
of her fingers.

"Big stupid dogs are capable of loyalty, and are a valuable
source of protein and companionship . . ." I began. She put the
car in gear.

"Before you go, one piece of intelligence from my under-
the-radar bombing run?"

"Yes, always have time for intelligence, particularly if it's
not work-related." She kept her foot on the brake.

"The cabin around the turn—Holly?"

"Yes, that's Josie and the judge."

"The judge isn't there," I said. "Someone else is. Someone
we know."

"Oh, no," said Emma, shaking her head. "I've got to talk to her." She rolled off down the hill without looking back.

■

I DID NOT WANT TO GET OUT of the lion's-paw tub in Laurel for a long time—pleasant memories, recent vintage—so I didn't.

I was dreading lunch; I felt I would be literally unable to face either Happy Gilliam or Josie Tillotson. Fortunately, neither was there. I thought of what my supervisor had told me when I was pulling an all-nighter before my first jury trial in the U.S. attorney's office in Brooklyn: whatever pressures you feel, however much you want to ask for a continuance, just remember the other side is feeling all those same pressures—and more, because you've got the white hat on. It's *United States v. Rantoul*, not *Rantoul v. Mullally*. Gilliam and Josie were doubtless either having bouillon cubes and saltines in separate cabins, or else they were two counties away by now.

Perhaps it was the weather putting a damper on people's spirits, but my sense was that during the sherry hour before lunch, the business and financial people in attendance were able to restrain their enthusiasm for Martha Holloway, their hostess.

"I can't believe this," said a man with dark sideburns and a string tie. Grazing rights activist, probably. "This is supposed to be a *Republican* administration, for God's sake.

"These staffers here have no more conception about how the business of the country is what makes this country work, than, than . . ."

I saw he would not soon or easily complete that sentence, so I moved on.

An upbeat murmur from the front door announced the vice president's arrival. As soon as she walked into the room, recrimination was forgotten and all parties in interest gathered round her like happy moths.

Holloway had evidently managed to outrun her umbrella-wielding Secret Service cohort, as she had plenty of rain in her hair. I fluttered over to her side.

She shook my hand. "Isn't this weather *glorious?*" she said. "It's a great day for sneaking up on the birds, put salt on their tails."

I nodded appreciatively. "It's a real duck day," I said.

"Great duck day," said she. "Just enough wind to keep 'em up and moving. Terrible upland day, though, they'd hang tighter than a tick in this rain, you'd have to kick 'em up."

The president of a large industrial concern, the not very bright president of a large industrial concern, decided at this point to contribute to our conversation. "Yes, lovely weather for ducks," he opined, and forced a laugh. Holloway turned her back on him, in the same motion grasping the elbow of a new arrival so that she could move him right along.

The vice president had never married, but there were no whispers about her sexual preference. She clearly enjoyed the company of men. There had been a suggestion or two during her race for governor that she enjoyed it rather a lot. Now her political adversaries in Washington insisted that she enjoyed the protection of her male Secret Service detail on a nightly basis, but Washington says that about every woman with a Secret Service detail, so it was impossible to know if there was any truth to it.

Here she conducted herself in a manner 100% fresh and businesslike, yet retaining some of the excitement of flirtation. It was all in her eyes, not in anything she said. Her transcripts would read well, I thought. I wondered if she was a role model for Sarah Blakeslee.

The crowd at lunch had thinned considerably from the day before. I finally made the A list and got seated at the veep's table. Wouldn't you know, though this was strictly a social occasion, sugar and soybeans did come up.

"Madam Vice President," Sam Burriss began, "we are all so grateful to you for taking the partisan tinge off this weekend by including so many representatives of the loyal opposition"—he raised a glass in my direction—"particularly such highly intelligent and well-informed members of the opposition as Senator Gilliam and Senator Mullally."

"You mean, who have the intelligence and information necessary to be with you on price supports," said Holloway good-naturedly. She called them "price supports," rather than "prass spoats," reminding me that most of Florida is a northern state.

"Precisely." Burriss laughed. "Our only wish is that your membership in the administration did not constrain you to embrace one of its very few wrongheaded initiatives."

"Well, I'm a loyal mem—, a full-fledged member of the administration, dues paid and in good standing, at least the last time I looked," Holloway began. Several of the lobbyists exchanged smug little glances to prove how smart they were.

How stupid is that? I asked myself. It doesn't get any stupider than that. You guys feel better? You think Martha Holloway is inattentive, that's why she's vice president of the United States and you're huckster salesmen? Remind me to invite you to Lanny's next poker game, so you can make yourselves feel better by letting us all know how good your cards are.

"But on this one," Holloway was saying as I snapped back into real time, "I'm more with the program than the program is. You want fertile soil here, maybe you should talk with my boss. The boss of us all," she added, looking around to approving smiles.

"It's difficult for the president to acknowledge the, uh, *complexities* of the situation when so much effort is devoted to oversimplifying the issue, making us look like Standard Oil of New Jersey," said Burriss, wheezing slightly.

"You mean, effort by me?"

"The media are only too happy to join in."

"I'm only telling you, Sam, you want a receptive audience on this, you're probably in the wrong place."

"I would suggest that means I'm in precisely the right place."

"Well, *I* would suggest that you're in the wrong place among other reasons because I told you last night I would see you in my office about this *and* the Everglades bill *after* lunch, not during it." She turned to me.

"In fact, Senator Mullally, why don't you join me and Sam in the study? I know you came out on his side on price supports, but you know I'm a big fan of your law enforcement record, your work with Phil Vacco, and you're good on the environment and there *is* the Everglades bill, and, well, maybe we can just talk some *sense* into each other! Or even into Sam, here." She placed her open palm onto Burriss's clenched fist, which rested to the left of her fish fork.

"I'd be delighted, Madam Vice President," I said. I realized there was something missing in everything she had said: smarmy code words.

Holloway turned the discussion to mixed bag hunting in her native Charlotte County: turkey, quail, dove, snipe, duck, javelina, and snake, all in the same outing. It sounded good to me, but the leaders of the industrial world, though I was sure they were all hunters, had other quarry on their minds. There was a lengthy minuet, in which they spoke of legislation and she of vegetation, at which point we were summoned to coffee in another room.

■

THE CROWD OVER THE DEMITASSES was even thinner—veep and Burriss being among the casualties. The wine had loosed a few more tongues.

"That lady could maybe be FLOTUS, but never POTUS," observed one, entirely too loudly. The straight-ahead stare of the Secret Service agent in the corner, not ten feet away, seemed to grow stonier than usual, if possible.

"I agree," said another.

"It's like, she never took off that prosecutor's hat. SEC, See Everything Crooked."

Whoa! Prosecutor Mullally, Señor Integridad, can't be standing idly by and listening to *this!* I took two steps away, felt a hand on my arm, and turned to see a familiar face.

"Dana Curran, Senator, Secret Service, the vice president will see you now. Won't you follow me, please."

She looked different without her trenchcoat.

Three turns later, Agent Curran opened a small mahogany door and I was face-to-face with the vice president.

"Welcome to my hideaway study," she said. "I promised Myron I would only read gothic novels in here, so he'd let me have it, ain't that right, Sam?"

Sam Burriss was seated in a comfortable chair facing the veep's desk. He did not look comfortable. Or happy. Evidently, this was a continuation of the ferocious standoff earlier.

After lunch, Sam, not during it. So the lady hadn't wanted to make a scene. But now she apparently did want at least one witness.

Holloway's voice was slow and stress-free. She was summing up.

"Sam, we've been around this barn so often we're about to meet ourselves. It does nobody any good for you to repeat your conclusion fifteen times, whether it's in public or in private. I am not stupid. I understand your organization's position. I understand the basis for it, and I understand that it is a rational position. And I don't want you to think that I am ungrateful for the support which you and individual members of your industry have given me over the years."

Burriss smiled. He was remembering that he had done his work well. The smile disappeared as Holloway pressed on.

"It's just that *you've* got to understand there is something on the other side, and that's the question of what kind of life do we want to have on this planet?

"*I* very much want to have the kind of life where I can wade through a slough with live oak and Spanish moss on either side of me, and put up eight different types of heron and egret along the way. I want to be able to sit under a mangrove or a cypress all day and be at one with my world.

"Now, unfortunately for your present position, these are preferences buried deep in my psyche, because they rest on my experiences as a little girl and a young woman in Charlotte and De Soto counties, great state of Florida. So my position here is not subject to change, short of a lobotomy or a life-altering experience which I truly do not anticipate and which I assure you *no* conversation with *you* is going to amount to." Sam's smile returned, rueful.

"We're both going to be sorry about this, Mattie," he said. She glared, evidently not appreciating the nickname, long out of use.

"Maybe, maybe not. I'm well aware your perception, over the years, has been that elected officials' views are indeed subject to change, depending upon the amount of financial support you are able to gather for their reelection campaigns. Your perception is not without evidentiary support. It's only that—"

"Madam Vice President, the stakes here for us are much higher than campaign contributions. The Everglades legislation, if it passed, would carry a price tag of thirty million dollars for my clients in the first year alone. That's a hell of a way to ring in the millennium. Now, Mattie—I am sorry, Madam Vice President—I have known you since you were that little girl you speak of, and you know I was a great friend of your daddy and I wish only a world full of blessings for his daughter, but we have got to be realistic about this. The interests I represent are not going to lie down and take a thirty-million-dollar-a-year hit and say thank you. It is simply not going to happen. And the fact is that you are the only major force agitating for this at the national level."

"Meaning?"

Burriss was flustered. "It means nothing more or less than what it says, than what I said."

Holloway's eyes narrowed. "Sam, let me make this easier for you. I am here to tell you, right now, that you may rely neither on hope nor on experience. I know what you guys are saying out there in the other room, and I have something to say to you in return: I am going to *crush* the sugarcane industry in the state of Florida if it is the last thing I ever do. If I have to use every bit of dirty laundry I've got on every single Senator—and believe me, my friend, I've got a hamperful, on each and every one—I will do it. I will be like a strangler fig on a saw palmetto. Remember the Justice Department prosecutors owe their positions to me in this administration, that's the dowry I insisted on, that and the judges. And if I have to go to that pig of a human being Harry Frobisch and tell him I'm just starting to remember things that Myron Brinker did during the campaign, and does he think I should share them with my girlfriends at the *Tribune*, I will do it. That, my friend, is leverage."

Burriss's mouth quivered; he looked honestly horrified.

"Finally, let me tell you something else, Sam. I know you represent more than sugar. And I know, much as you would love to clear-cut the entire Everglades, it's even more important to you to grab billions of dollars from the taxpayers every year and put it right into the pockets of your so-called 'agribusiness' clients. That's a big laugh, by the way: they're *all* John D. Rockefeller and Big Jim Fisk to me. So here's something to think about: if you don't drop your opposition to my Everglades bill, and I mean *drop*, I will personally see to it that you and your clients are screwed, blewed, and tattooed on every price support in the United States Code. They'll all be gone, Sam. Not too many people could make that happen, but I can. Not too many people can make the administration hurt bad from the inside, instead of just trying to scare the little pigs by huffing and puffing from the outside. I can."

I had heard worse, maybe, but only between prosecutor and defense lawyer. And only defense lawyers who are former prosecutors, otherwise you'd see the whole conversation between the covers of an affidavit in support of a motion to dismiss the indictment.

Burriss evidently hadn't heard worse, or even as good. He was ashen, trembling. "You, you can't do that," he sputtered. "You, you can't *say* that!"

"I just did, honey." She drummed her fingers on the desk. Evidently a signature gesture.

"But, but, you're the vice"—he gasped for breath—*"president* of the *United States.* You can't threaten people. That's extortion!" He stood up precipitously, spilling coffee from his demitasse onto the pale rug, and in his haste set the dripping cup on Holloway's mahogany desk. He bolted from the room. "The vice president can't *do* that!" he cried on his way out, though it was not clear whether he was whining to us or to himself.

Holloway was looking straight ahead, frowning. She sighed. I didn't move.

"Well," she finally said. "That was pleasant." She pushed her chair back, rose, and placed her hand on the knob of the door behind her, then looked at me. I was sitting on the sofa like an idiot, wishing I was a thousand miles away.

"Sometimes," she said, "sometimes you wish you could turn the clock back five minutes, don't you?"

I shrugged.

"Extortion under color of official right. Twenty years, isn't it?"

I nodded. "Or they could say Section 201, seeking a thing of value," I said. "That's fifteen years. I wouldn't worry about Sam, though. He doesn't seem like a man to rock the boat."

"I'm not worried about Sam," said Martha Holloway, looking straight at me.

She shook her head, opened the door and was gone, leaving former assistant U.S. attorney Terrence Mullally, Jr., a member of the supposedly hated opposition bloc in the Senate, alone in her study, with her unlocked desk and its carpet of official papers. I didn't see any gothic novels, and I didn't look. I left the room the way I had come in, and I didn't even compose my features for the benefit of the Secret Service. I just walked out. That's what she had done.

I had gone only a few steps when it hit me: now I had another prize I could bring to Anson Vivian's table. A real broadsword. Should be worth a lot, clanging down on that table.

But might be worth more in the scabbard.

Not to Vivian, of course.

Part Nine

Monday morning behind my desk, I was daydreaming about Martha Holloway handling copperheads during a church prayer session. They were twined around her arms, even her neck. Naturally, I jumped when the phone rang. It was Lanny.

"I got your pal Phil Vacco here, Boss, calling in, line three."

"Terry Mullally."

"Senator, it's Phil Vacco. I need to have a, I need to have some time with you, for a, ah, to go over some things."

"Nothing easier. Come right over, we are at your disposal, I have a gallon of the Republic of Colombia's finest, rock sugar, you will not be disappointed . . ."

"Senator, this is my business, not your business."

He had addressed me twice by my title. That should have sent my antennae way up. I was not functioning as a major league player. This was crazy. I was getting spooked. Events were pinwheeling. Best to extend, delay, get into another news cycle. Tomorrow's headlines would sweep this away, whatever it was. . . .

"Oh, okay, your business. Meaning?"

"Meaning we have to meet in my office, not your office, or we'll both be answering a lot of questions."

I knew what this meant. Grand jury would be looking at everything, including what was happening right now.

"Sure, I can drop over on my way to the Humphrey Center, should I bring anybody, anybody knowledgeable on a specific topic?"

"No, just your bright smiling self."

I attempted to pour my discombobulated self into my bright smiling self, and decided to walk, not ride, down the hill to Pennsylvania and Tenth. Didn't feel like company.

The guards at Justice whisked me by without making me go through the metal detector, which pleased me because I knew it was a violation of their rules. I nodded to let them know that I appreciated this.

I walked the length of the corridor to Tenth and Constitution, listening to the echo of my own heavy and important footsteps, feeling more chipper by the minute. I bounded up the stairs to the second floor, two at a time, and at the top nearly wiped out a small woman who had just gripped the rail to go down. I steadied her.

"I'm terribly sorry, I—oh, hi!" It was Marian Stultz of the *Tribune.* "What are you doing here?"

"I'm just a working girl reporter trying to make a living, Senator. What are *you* doing here?"

"Phil Vacco and I are old friends and colleagues from Boston, from the prosecutor's office there, and of course as you know off the record from the other evening, we have some of the same jurisdiction on the independent prosecutor thing." Was this going to be good enough for Marian?

Yes. "No one said that was off the record, Senator."

"Marian, it was a *dinner party,* for heaven's sake. Is nothing sacred? Don't answer that."

She laughed. "Not much, I'm afraid, but maybe dinner parties is one of them. We working girls like to feed and be fed."

"I do appreciate that. Remember, we fed you! Anyway, we'll see you in court, Ms. Stultz." I smiled.

"See you in court, Senator." She smiled.

I was still smiling as I crested the stairs and crossed the corridor, just in case anyone was looking. Nixon got caught on camera letting a phony smile drop and then revving it up for the next customer. Very bad visual, particularly when preserved in a ten-second spot and run at twelve hundred gross rating points a week, the month before the election. I was thinking ahead, thinking around corners. Maybe I was getting the hang of this town after all.

But I had to think about the present, too. Think grand jury. What the hell is the grand jury doing? It's a question you're not allowed to ask.

I marched briskly but deferentially—a lot of raw power here—into the cavernous reception area for the chief of the Criminal Division. Three of the four secretaries in the outer chamber raced over to greet me. As Phil Vacco's initial patron in public life, I was a hero in this office.

From behind the closed door to Phil's office, forty feet of carpeting away, I could hear animated voices, male and female. Mary Jane and Ellen and Gladys, all veterans of the Criminal Division, led me to the other end of the reception area, made their greetings voluble, asked me questions, brought me coffee, and generally blotted out any word I might have picked up from within. Mary Jane returned to her desk and I noticed her smile stayed in place as she buzzed to say that Senator Mullally was here.

The door opened. Phil Vacco and two aides emerged and walked over to me.

"Senator, so good of you to come on such short notice. May I introduce my special assistants, Anthony Vidaly and Susan Schutter. Tony, you remember, was with me in the U.S. attorney's office in Boston, and Susan is on loan from the Tax Division."

"Ah, yes," I said, clapping Vidaly on the shoulder and pumping the hand of the young woman. "Love those *Klein* conspiracies." She groaned—was it possible she was not a people person?

Phil quickly put in, "Yes, we do, we do love those *Klein* conspiracies." *Klein* conspiracies are tax conspiracies. They're nearly impossible to defend against. I had murdered people with them in the Brooklyn office.

We marched into Phil's enormous office and took seats around the butler's table. I had been in here a couple of times when I was an assistant U.S. attorney in Brooklyn, once on narcotics and once on a police corruption case, and things looked different.

"I see you've rearranged, you've moved the desk," I said. Susan Schutter groaned again. My take was she wanted to treat me, and everyone else in the world, as an arm's-length enemy, and she resented this reminder of prior shared experience.

She was carrying an accordion folder with reams of memos sticking out, many covered with a pink or red jacket indicating the degree of security clearance required to read the contents. I decided to let her have a jab.

"So, Ms. Schutter, I see you're working on a lot of confidential and top secret material." I gave her a smile. Everyone could see, however, that this meant "lighten up."

"Oh, that's from another case," she said, and placed the folder behind her chair, where I could no longer see it. Amateur night.

"Another *case?* This is a case?" I turned to Phil.

His eyes were relaxed. Phil was a pro. "We just have to ask you a few questions, Senator."

"Should I get a lawyer? You can't be too careful, you know." I made it plain I was joking. Of course I was not.

"We've discussed that, and we don't think it will be necessary at this time," said Nurse Ratched. I smiled again and began thinking about how I could get her fired.

This pleasing train of thought was interrupted by Phil Vacco.

"It concerns two of your favorite topics, Asian organized crime and New York cops."

"Oh, so you want me as an expert witness?"

"Just the facts, ma'am, just the facts." Vacco shook his head.

"It will not surprise you to learn," he went on, "that the Southeast Asian heroin traffickers have been attempting to pay off virtually every law enforcement officer they can find in New York City. While in most cases the line has held, they have enjoyed some success."

Phil looked at me. So did the two special assistants. I was

paying attention, no smiles, all business. This had, after all, been my line of work, both as an assistant in Brooklyn and later as the district attorney in Boston.

"Among other things, the investigation has focused on an officer who joined the department in 1995, after you had left the U.S. attorney's office to go to Boston. He did narcotics work with Lieutenant Rudy Solano, who you had done a number of cases with in the early nineties—"

"And who is not around to discuss them," I said glumly.

"And who died at that hunting camp in New Hampshire in November 1997, coroner's verdict suicide."

"I testified at the inquest," I said.

Ms. Schutter could not resist proving how smart she was. "We know, we have the transcript." She began to reach around behind her before realizing that producing the transcript would show she had lied—er, fibbed—about the contents of the accordion folder. So she awkwardly scratched her shoulder and looked away. I made a mental note to invite her, too, to Lanny's next poker game.

Vacco broke the silence. "Relevance is this, Senator. Cop is a bad cop, we've got him six ways to Sunday, could take him down tomorrow, but he's talking rather freely to a number of people whom we've already turned, or whose conversations we are privy to."

I held up my hand in front of my face. "Okay, okay, I don't need the details." I knew Phil could not be more specific about wiretaps without violating the confidentiality provisions of Title III, the federal electronic surveillance law. For a prosecutor to disclose the contents of a wiretap is a felony, and one the feds sometimes take seriously. Of course, if we had been alone, I would have tried to get it out of him anyway, just not in mixed company.

"Bottom line is this," said Phil. "Officer X claims to have been sharing money with Rudy Solano for the entire three years they overlapped. And that's not all he has to say about the late lieutenant. Says he was involved up to his eyeballs in Operation Submarine, that nice case where you and Rod Owen took down the six dirty cops and the three gay bar owners, but Solano was never charged."

I maintained an expression of professional interest as my mind raced. Vacco was not telling me anything I didn't know, but how much of this was I *supposed* to know?

"Our man's account is independently corroborated by a bad guy recently returned to this area from the Far East. Says Solano was on the take forever. Remember, this allegation came up in your Senate campaign and it kind of washed out?"

"Yes, yes, of course I remember. Senator Dellenbach had the whole goddamn federal government in New York City trying to prove Rudy Solano was a crook and therefore I was a crook, and they couldn't come up with anything, if memory serves."

"They weren't the executive branch, they didn't have electronic surveillance on Solano or anybody else," said Phil. "At any rate, this bad guy, who was in custody in Hong Kong until recently, he says not only did he split dough with Rudy, but he thinks Rudy was murdered. No firsthand knowledge, he was incarcerated over there at the time, but he talks a good game."

I knew I could no longer sit like a cigar-store Indian and let this one pass by. I jumped up, jabbing my thumb into my chest.

"*I'm* the one, I was the *only* one, who said I didn't think Rudy would have committed suicide!" I shouted.

"We know, we know," said Phil. Nurse Ratched nodded too. She had studied the transcript of the inquest.

"Let me ask you something else," I hurried on. "Is the name of your pal by any chance Cooper?"

Phil's expression didn't change, so I looked around at the other two. Tony was okay, game face, but Susan Schutter's jaw was halfway to the floor. Give me a library-stacks tax lawyer every time for free discovery of what the other side has. Now I knew what I had to do.

"Reason I ask is, I got this crazy call a couple of weeks ago from a guy, sounded Asian, said he knew Rudy Solano and Paul

Slifka and a guy named Cooper, who I never heard of. Said his name was Reed, or Ring, I think. I wasn't sure if he was a nut."

I expected this would mark the beginning of a set of explanations, a lengthy account of the telephone conversation, which I was not looking forward to. Instead, Phil suddenly stood up. What the hell was going on?

"Okay, I think that's enough for today," he said. "Thank you, Susan, thank you, Tony." They were out of the room, with their files, without a glance in my direction. I turned to follow them and Phil put a hand on my shoulder. "Have a seat, Terry," he said.

I sat down. I was studying Phil and he was studying me. It was becoming clear I was operating at a hopeless information deficit. Best thing to do in that situation is to say nothing, don't show what cards you have or don't have.

■

AFTER WHAT SEEMED LIKE TEN MINUTES but was probably closer to ten seconds, Phil leaned back in his chair and exhaled.

"Our only purpose this morning was to see if you would report that conversation. You passed the test, thank God."

"Oh?"

"We picked up that call to your office, in real time. We've got a roving tap on Olie Wing."

"Olie Wing! For Chrissakes, Phil, Olie Wing is a hit man! Was he the guy who called? Olie Wing is all kinds of dangerous. *He's* calling my Senate office? He killed his own bodyguard, left him dead in an alley, a .22-caliber shot to the neck, point-blank, after the bodyguard had wasted two lowlife—"

Phil held up his hand. "We know all about it, Terry, trust me, we know all about it. We have all the files from all of your

cases and it all checks out. Olie is a very bad fellow. But time
has not stood still since you left the U.S. attorney's office. We
now have even more information than you did back in 1994.
And some of that information is not flattering to Solano, which
is why we're not laughing hysterically when we hear our Hong
Kong wet boy claim Solano may have been bumped off. Nothing definite, just where there's smoke, you know?"

"Yeh. I don't blame you. Served me well over the years, I
can tell you that."

"You don't have to, you don't have to. Remember, I was
right there with you for two of those years."

"So you were, my friend, so you were." I let Phil see me
taking a couple of deep breaths.

"Now why is it," I began, "that Ms. Schutter so obviously
wants to indict my rear end into the middle of next week?"

Phil laughed. "She thinks all elected officials are crooks,
nothing personal."

"Can I show her my tax returns? I make less money and
pay more taxes than anybody I know."

"She'd probably find a typo and indict you for that. We've
got it under control. She's just here for the IRS stuff, not the police corruption stuff. But I needed to have her and Tony see that
you would tell us about the telephone call, as I was sure you
would. There was, candidly, a little bit of angst over here when
you didn't report it immediately, and even more angst when you
didn't come up with it last Saturday, at Camp David. I had told
them I thought you would. That was a scripted conversation,
though not wired, we wouldn't do that to a sitting senator without probable cause. So I had to let the staffers here see for themselves. Particularly Sue Schutter, who, uh, doesn't report to me."

"Phil, I didn't know who the hell the caller was, and it's
also not like I don't have anything else going on, I don't work
for the goddamn Department of Justice anymore. I—"

"Relax, relax. That one's all over for now. I'll let you know
if I need anything more. I just had to let you sink or swim on
your own."

"And these are shark-infested waters," I observed.

Phil sipped one of the five unfinished mugs of coffee on his desk. Must have been an early morning.

"Speaking of sharks," he said, "our friends in the fourth estate seem awfully eager for us to empanel a grand jury to investigate fund-raising parties, both at the Humphrey Center and the Reagan Center. Any expert opinion there, whether it's smoke or fire?"

I grimaced and shook my head. So Marian Stultz was feeding. "They all love to cover parties, because they can write about the champagne and caviar and blackened tuna and a lot of stuff John Q. and Susie Q. don't see every day, and that gets the reading public all steamed up. But it's basically a cheap shot. The most you'll find at those parties is Darlene from Abilene paid a grand to come, and either before or after that she got a special bonus of fifteen hundred or two grand from her boss, who just happens to work for the timber industry or whatever. The real scandal, from where I sit, is soft money to the national parties—corporate and unlimited. That's where I'd take my subpoena."

"Sounds like pretty good advice."

"Well, that advice, at least, is experience-based."

"The public can always use men of experience to help guide its affairs," said Phil. "That's a point I've heard the vice president make on more than one occasion, recently."

This clearly was not an idle comment. I looked at Phil and saw nothing in his face, no give, no giveaway. "What do you think she means by that?" I asked nonchalantly.

"Well, you know, she's always on the lookout for talent, she loves controlling the appointment of the U.S. attorneys and district judges, feels she's making a real contribution there. Fact is, she's let me know that if I don't fall on my face here, I can probably look forward to a district judgeship in either Boston or Washington before the end of the term, and if she's still around after 2000, I can look forward to being elevated to the circuit."

"I thought her deal with Frobisch and Brinker was she gets only the district level."

"It is. If she's still around after 2000, it wouldn't be as number two, it would only be as number one."

"You think they'd drop her from the ticket?"

"They won't have to. She thinks Frobisch is corrupt, has told him so to his face. She won't run with them again. Knows too much, she says."

"She confides in you?"

"For some reason."

"Emma and I thought she was great, at Camp David. Did you suggest she include us?"

"No, that was her idea. She has been an admirer of yours, from a distance, and now of Emma, too. She wants to do a one-on-one lunch with Emma and talk more about anthropology."

"Emma would love that."

We stared at the fireplace.

"If she goes all the way, you could do considerably better than district judge, Terry. In all candor."

"I'm a Democrat."

"Not a problem. I've even heard her discuss it. It would prove she was nonpartisan, depoliticizing the Justice Department, the criminal justice process. Remember?"

I did remember. This had been my constant refrain during nine years as a prosecutor. I moved over to the mantelpiece and inspected a string of Japanese netsuke, little ivory carvings. I picked one up, a grotesque monkey, and turned it over. It had a fat, smooth tummy.

"Sounds good to me," I said.

Two good reasons to be a federal appeals judge, was always the word in the Department of Justice. July and August.

■

WASHINGTON IS AN EARLIER TOWN than Boston, so I usually have my daily staff meeting at 8:00 A.M., an hour sooner than when I was district attorney in Suffolk County, Massachusetts. The Boston reporters like to sleep in—don't get me wrong, I agree with them—whereas the Washington reporters prefer to get a quicker jump on the daily task of ruination.

Lanny and Jerry and Bull Flannery were waiting for me in the conference room when I checked in at 7:57 A.M. on Tuesday, July 27.

"Big buzz, huge buzz, Boss," Lanny muttered. "Something major today, blot out the sun on the noon news. Minority view, it's from Treasury, consensus is Justice."

"How can a buzz have a consensus? Where's it from?"

Jerry waved her hand. "All around, all around. Cannot be a mistake. Something big coming."

"I'm not sure I like the sound of this." I punched 514-2601. Mary Jane picked up on the first ring.

"Good morning, Miss Brickley, this is Terry Mullally calling. I wondered if the assistant attorney general is by any chance around and available?"

"Certainly, Senator." Four seconds later, I heard "Phil Vacco." I shook my head. I love efficiency.

"Phil, Terry. Something major out of DOJ today, this morning?"

"Off the record, *way* OTR, noon news is the outlet, all networks, just watch, you'll get it same time as everybody else, I'm recused from the whole matter, you'll understand when you see it."

"Any hints?"

"My lips are sealed tighter than a FISA application."

I chuckled. Probably fifteen people in the world would have appreciated this reference to the ultraclassified Foreign Intelligence Surveillance Act, way beyond codeword.

"Sounds like it could be a hair-curdling development," was Bull Flannery's take.

Lanny held up a forefinger. "Other thing is, Boss, political people for Honorable Gilliam and Honorable Vivian still very attentive to your desires, daily basis, still hanging on, rather, waiting for, your every word, each would love you to put him out of his misery, declare yourself, etc."

"*Gilliam* is still calling for my *support?*"

"Says he expects it. So does Vivian."

"I am sure," I said. These were not positive words, from me. "Well? What am I to do?"

"Nothing."

"Good. That's what I do best."

"We know," said both Lanny and Jerry.

"What's my outside time frame?"

"Your outside outside time frame is the day before the New Hampshire primary, which would be February 14 of next year. Realistically, if you want to get substantial credit, your outside time frame is probably Labor Day."

"Why would I want to get some credit?"

"You wouldn't, unless you want to be in the Cabinet, which you don't—"

"Or at least we don't want you to be," Jerry explained.

"So I should just sit tight?"

Lanny and Jerry and Bull all nodded. "You don't want to make a move," advised Bull, "until that train is about to sail."

"I'll wait 'til noon, anyway," I said. "Maybe Gilliam and Vivian are both about to be indicted. Or me, it could be me." I laughed at my own joke. Staff wasn't amused. Too close to the bone.

ALL THE TV NETWORKS had somehow simultaneously tumbled onto the same story just in time for their respective noon broadcasts: that the Justice Department had opened a hush-hush formal investigation of allegations that Martha Holloway, the vice president of the United States, had under color of her office committed extortion, a twenty-year felony, upon the person of a registered legislative agent in Washington, D.C.

"What does all this teach us, Cheri?" asked one desk anchor.

Cheri, from the north lawn of the White House, had no hesitation: "Well, Turc, I hate to put it this way, but it suggests that no matter who you are, if you lie down with lobbyists, you get fleas."

I squinted at the TV and could make out a thousand fleas buzzing around Cheri's perfectly coiffed head. I wondered how you would calculate the odds of Martha Holloway lying down with Sam Burriss. It's a round number, anyway. "This is very bad," I said.

"Because we like Holloway?" asked Jerry.

"Because I think I'm a witness," I said. "I was right there when the veep was having a screaming match with a guy who meets the description. At Camp David."

"Witness for the prosecution, or for the defense?" asked Bull Flannery.

I stared at him. "I don't know enough about the facts to say," I said. Meaning, don't hurry me to decide that. Whereupon the topic was dropped.

"This is unbelievable," said Lanny. "Brinker is in *Turkey*. How secure do you think the phone line was when Frobisch laid this all out for him? It doesn't get any more secure than that. This had to come straight from Brinker. That's it, he's running, this is as good as an announcement speech. She's out, so he has to run, save the Party and the country from those irresponsible Democrats, etc. It's so obvious. Will nothing make you sick?"

"Cute," said Bull Flannery. "Cute as a shithouse rat."

No mixed metaphor there.

I called Phil Vacco. "What gives?" was all I said.

"Much as I don't want to discuss this over the telephone, I even more cannot be seen talking with you now in person, this thing could even move over to your end of the Avenue, who knows?" This meant impeachment.

"Off off off, the request to open an investigation came here, I recused myself—had to, veep pulled out all the stops to put me here—and it thereafter went through the department like suet through a goose, skipped the fourth floor"—this was a reference to Deputy Attorney General Buffington—"vetted

and signed in jig time on the fifth floor." This was a reference
to the attorney general's chambers. "Never seen anything like
it. Disgusting. None of those guys would know a criminal case
if it bit them in the ass, here they're making high-wire decisions, and gleefully so, in five minutes. No fact-checking, no
legal analysis, nothing: just an uncorroborated assertion by a
lobbyist, and they say, 'Oh, okay, we're over the rail on *that*
one!' If they'd applied that standard earlier in the year, they'd
all be in jail themselves."

"You don't sound like an entirely happy camper, Philip
my lad."

"I'll feel better in the morning. No, strike that."

I laughed. Mistake.

"By the way," he added. "The internal memo lists you as a
witness. Apparently you were right there, for one of the conversations at least. Congratulations, you're at the center of attention. Isn't that good?"

Phil was busting my chops. We both knew what happens
to people in those circumstances. They spend the rest of their
lives trying to live down or forget those fifteen minutes in the
national spotlight.

"Yes, of course that's always good," I said.

"One more thing you might want to know," said Phil.

"Yes?"

"The vice president has scheduled a press conference for
four o'clock."

■

FOR TODAY, KEY WITNESS THOUGH I might prove to be, I
was safe from the press. Today belonged to Martha Holloway.
There was not a camera, not a reporter in sight as Lanny and
Jerry and I walked down the hill along Pennsylvania to the Em-

pire Grill, a law enforcement watering hole, for a mind-clearing luncheon of duck and wine.

Every time I go to the Empire Grill, I expect to bump into Jay Gould or some other robber baron of the Gilded Age. There are Tiffany lamps and brass railings everywhere, buffalo heads aplenty, and lots of frosted glass partitions so you can't see the other diners. Virtually every table seems to be in a private and cozy nook. The layout of the place is an invitation to debauch or connivance.

We had asked for the bill and were enjoying three of Anson Vivian's Montecristos when the maître d' materialized in our corner and said in a low voice that a gentleman at the bar had asked if he could join us for just a moment. He handed me a card: WILLIAM P. TREMBLAY, PRIVATE INVESTIGATOR. SPECIAL AGENT, UNITED STATES SECRET SERVICE (RETIRED).

I handed the card to Jerry. "Sound like your type? Every time you light up a cigar, the men come running." There was some truth to this, and Jerry blushed.

"Amazing what will make some people blush," Lanny said. He looked at the card, turned to the maître d', and said, "Sure, show him over."

Our caller was a paunchy, worried-looking man of about sixty. He had had the good grace to leave his gin at the bar, but it hung on his breath. We had been mistaken as to his intentions.

"Senator, in performing work for a client, I have come into possession of information that is relevant to the investigative subcommittee which you chair. I had been thinking of approaching your office, but was not certain how to get through to you. I would like to share this information with you, in confidence. These are members of your staff?"

"My two closest."

"Your charge, as I understand it, is to determine why the attorney general has not applied for independent prosecutors to investigate suggestions of conflict of interest or corruption on the part of members of the Brinker administration."

"Your understanding is correct."

"He has not because he cannot. The attorney general and two members of the Cabinet—all inner circle advisers during the 1996 campaign—have apparently arranged for substantial sums of money to be transferred by campaign donors to off-shore investment accounts."

I remembered the expression on Senator Gilliam's face when I had trashed Harry Frobisch, at the Pied de Mouton. So maybe they're not just two peas in a pod, maybe they're two chicks in a nest egg. A growing nest egg. Better not look too interested.

"Doesn't sound illegal so far. Frobisch do anything for these donors? His name on the accounts?"

"It may not be illegal yet, but Frobisch has done plenty for these guys, for a long time, and is still doing so. These donors are much more sophisticated, financially, than Harry Frobisch is. They hardly need to coordinate with him in setting up off-shore investment accounts, unless there's an anticipation of something happening down the road. Furthermore, I have reason to believe that Frobisch, who doesn't have a pot to piss in, has nonetheless set up an offshore account of his own in the same tax haven jurisdiction."

"Well, that's at least interesting, even if not illegal, but what does 'reason to believe' mean?"

"Can't get at the records, my hunch is it's Caymans or Bermuda. Only thing I'm certain of is Frobisch and those two Cabinet guys are going to walk away from this as rich men. And unless there's an independent investigation, nobody will ever know about it. This is what that leaked story about Simon Buffington is getting at, but it doesn't stop at Buffington. That's why they have to stonewall."

"Your *hunch?*"

The man whose card said Tremblay nodded.

"Your source?"

He shook his head. "Client. Can't come forward. For one thing, he'd need not just immunity but anonymity, which I've been around long enough to know nobody in this town can give him. He'd be instantly ruined."

"Thanks. I'll keep your card, and we'll give you a call if it becomes appropriate."

"Thank you, Senator." He nodded at Lanny and Jerry and left. Never tried to sit down in the fourth chair, never shook my hand. Man in a hurry. Left his drink at the bar.

"I liked him," Jerry said.

"I think maybe his name really is Tremblay," said Lanny.

I put my fists on the table and leaned forward.

"Sounds like maybe Harry Frobisch's actual crimes aren't long behind him," I said. "Sounds like maybe they're a couple of years in front of him."

■

I CALLED PHIL VACCO AS SOON AS WE GOT BACK to the office. I had learned my lesson. Fool me once, shame on you; fool me twice, shame on me.

Mary Jane said Mr. Vacco was at the White House. "President call him in?" I asked, not thinking fully.

"He's with the vice president," she replied briskly. "I'll have the driver tell him to give you a call as soon as he gets back in the car."

"Land line would be preferable. Friendly land line." Those official car phones are not only insecure; at Phil Vacco's level of sensitivity, they're often tapped by authority of the White House—for "security reasons," of course.

"Understood."

Phil got back to me at quarter past three. "I'm in the office, on the red phone," he said.

"Name William Tremblay mean anything to you?" I asked.

"Oh God, is he off the reservation? He's been here, he's one of our sources on the investment pool stuff, but only one, and he's frustrated the department hasn't wrapped the thing up months ago. I'm new, but that's invisible to him. Terry, you can't go public with him, it would blow our whole operation prematurely, before we're ready, it would probably burn a couple of sources Tremblay doesn't even know about, they'd roll up the net in no time. More to the point, nothing illegal has been done yet, they're just setting it up."

"You're investigating the attorney general of the United States as well as Happy Gilliam?"

"Yes. You didn't need to know that. You should hear it and forget it."

"Does the attorney general know that?"

"No."

"Does the president know it?"

"No."

I didn't really need to ask the next question, but I went ahead anyway.

"Does the vice president know it?"

"Yes. And if we develop enough admissible evidence to apply for an independent prosecutor, the whole world will know it. Because I personally will tell them. On that one, everyone above me in the department will be recused, so I will be the acting attorney general. No one can order me to stop."

"Lovely weather we're having, Philip."

"Lovely weather."

Part Ten

THE VICE PRESIDENT HELD HER 4:00 P.M. press conference in the presidential briefing room in the West Wing. She made no reference to the leaked story about the extortion investigation. Instead, with the eyes of the country and the world upon her, she announced she had come to a decision: she would be a candidate for the Republican presidential nomination in the year 2000.

We were watching it live. "Another nice move," said Lanny. "Always accelerate before a collision. These folks are really getting up there on the high wire."

Jerry was shaking her head admiringly. "Perfect move. Now it's going to be, 'Frobisch who?' and 'What about Brinker? He said he probably wouldn't run, didn't he?' "

The first question for Holloway after her prepared announcement was, "Does President Brinker know you are using the White House briefing room for this occasion?"

The answer was, "No. Next question."

"Madam Vice President, pardon me, but isn't this clearly a desperate move on your part to distract attention from the criminal investigation of your activities that has reportedly been opened?"

Holloway eyed the man scornfully. "Honey, anybody with subpoena power can open an investigation. They don't need to ask anybody. I used to be a federal prosecutor, I can tell you that. The hard part is finishing up the investigation with a conviction, and nothing like that's going to happen here, because these boys don't have any evidence, and wouldn't know what to do with it if they did."

"Do you suspect politics is behind this story?"

"Is money green? Of course, it's all politics."

An unshaven owlish man with a pencil behind his ear could contain himself no longer at this. He pushed the woman in front of him aside and stepped to the fore, pointing with his pencil: "Why do you say money and not grass? It's usually 'Is grass green?' Are you referring to the allegations against Simon Buffington, the secret bank accounts?"

"Sir, you are entitled to your interpretation. As a matter of fact, you're welcome to it." This got a laugh at the expense of the owlish man.

"Who is that guy?" I asked Jerry.

"Stringer. Unaffiliated, just tries to peddle crazy stuff to very small or lazy radio stations. Huge chip on his shoulder. He got bounced last year and sued to get his credentials back. Everybody hates him."

"Hard to see why, he carries himself so well," said Lanny.

The fellow now saw he was in a corner and lashed out: "Do you blame the media for blowing the extortion story out of proportion? It was obviously just a leak from Justice, the networks were spoon-fed . . ." He glared around him. Everyone else looked straight ahead, at Martha Holloway.

The vice president fidgeted with her pearls, sighed, and turned a look of compassion on the miserable reporter: "I never blame anybody for anything, except myself sometimes, when I've messed up. I just play the cards I'm dealt. As for this *ludicrous* account of what a bunch of Keystone Kops are hallucinating about, why I'm glad to see it out there! The more information I can get about what Harry Frobisch is up to, the better I like it. Now if you-all will excuse me, I've got a presidential campaign to attend to, and a few calls to make. Thanks very much for coming." She pivoted and was gone.

"Whew!" said Lanny.

"That's a piece of horseflesh," said Bull Flannery.

Myself, I thought of Ruthie Truslow, the amateur primatologist, tossing back a glass of red wine and announcing her conclusion: *Men and women aren't that different, they all have it in them.*

■

Mᴙ FIRST CALL, twenty minutes after Holloway's press conference ended, was from Ruthie's friend Tom Fenster, cream of the D.C. politigation bar. He didn't want anything, just wanted us to know he and his outfit represented my good friend Sam Burriss, and the American agricultural interests aligned with him. Had so much enjoyed dinner at our house with Ruth, he'd actually secured this engagement through Senator Gilliam, whom he'd met there, he was grateful for that, Ruth was having a blast with Emma long-distance, both Fenster and his clients were looking forward to the proceedings in the extortion case, should be interesting, quite a tale to tell, a bunch of history, prior dealings I might or might not be aware of, if I would like to discuss any of this, not my expected testimony of course, just get some of the *background*, Fenster could have a couple of tabbed binders run over to my office in five minutes, messenger was standing by, three hundred pages or so but four-page executive summary, very clear, helpful. Fenster would be available on no notice, with or without his three associates who were also familiar with the matter, whatever our preference, any time in the coming weeks. . . . I thanked him and rang off.

"I thought I read he was trying that big campaign finance case up in Baltimore," I said to Lanny.

"His partner took it over, he's grounded here for the foreseeable future with Soybeans, Incorporated."

"Shall we take delivery on the binders?" I asked.

"I'd say no. I wouldn't put it past them to leak the juiciest

part and say we said it. That way when we deny it, we're holding the documents that say it, that's close enough for a couple
TV stations and at least one newspaper I can think of."

"Let's take them anyway, I want to romance these guys."

"Why do you want to romance them? Boss, you're not
going for the microskirts, I hope."

"No, I just want to romance 'em real . . . slow."

Bull Flannery looked puzzled. Not Lanny.

"Ah," he said. "I see. Until it's too late."

I held a finger to my lips and gave everyone my innocent
expression. Even Bull understood this, and laughed.

"You may want to ask Tom Fenster a few 'preliminary' or
'procedural' questions halfway through your review, to freeze
them in place," said Jerry.

"Good thought," I said. Jerry was getting more twisted by
the day, really growing into her job.

The next fifteen calls were from the media, wanting to
know what my testimony was going to be and also, on background, what the topics and questions were going to be. What
was this about, anyway, what *was* the Hobbs Act? Jerry told
them of course we can't comment "because there's an actual or
potential pending investigation," which means nothing, but
they liked the sound of it, seemed sinister, so most of them re-
ported her quote and went away.

Two other calls were not so easily fobbed off: Happy
Gilliam and Anson Vivian. Both noted the battle lines were
now drawn for 2000, with a declared Republican in the race,
and earnestly sought my open support on political, practical,
philosophical, and metaphysical grounds. Gilliam on culinary
grounds, too. Both also insisted on knowing what the exact
substance of my testimony regarding the Camp David show-
down between Holloway and Burriss would be.

I used the second inquiry as a shield against the first. As to
Holloway-Burriss, I told my leaders that I had "been in touch
with the Justice Department," which was literally true, and that
I had been asked not to discuss my testimony, which was impossible to disprove.

Vivian pretended to be persuaded by this—I don't think he was fooled for a minute—but Happy Gilliam kept pressing.

"Believe me, my friend," I finally said to him, "you don't want to go anywhere near the edge when one of these investigations picks up a head of steam. It's just not worth it. The career people at Justice think every inquiry is an attempt to coordinate alibis and get a phony story straight. They think every gesture of support is witness-tampering, and if the person is not a witness, then it's an obstruction of justice anyway. You can't win, with these folks. I know whereof I speak, they're my folks! And the young political appointees, the Alexander Hamilton Society crowd, are even worse, because they don't know what the hell they're doing."

"Yes, I have observed that expertise to be a major arrow in your quiver," observed Gilliam. "One which can be used for defensive as well as offensive purposes, I suppose."

"Happy, I'm not defending anything, I have nothing to defend. All I'm going to do is follow my own advice to clients: 'Tell the truth, that way you don't have to remember what you said.' Anyone who has nothing to fear from the truth has nothing to fear from me.

"As for the presidential race, I think you'll agree, on analysis, that given the delicacy of my position as a fact witness, it will be better if I don't take on any partisan political coloration until, until Martha's hash is settled one way or the other." I winked at Senator Gilliam over the telephone. "We wouldn't want the public to get confused, wouldn't want criminal justice dust to get rubbed on the presidential campaign," I leered. "On your presidential campaign," I added, not wanting him to miss my point. Silence.

"Rest assured, I won't talk to Anson about 2000 without talking with you. I've told him the same thing." This was true—a winning and homely detail, sure to be checked.

My left-right combination led my two suitors to agree to suspend our conversations until after my testimony. Did they trust me? Let me put it this way: Lanny was told by their administrative assistants that Gilliam and Vivian had compared notes on every word I said. Lucky I know how to keep a story straight.

■

NO ONE WAS SURPRISED when the leadership scheduled an "emergency" session of the Senate for eight o'clock that evening. The roller coaster was picking up speed, and it was important to hold on tight. Best way to hold on is to be seen on national TV, prime time, making grave speeches and doing serious stuff.

"Where are you going?" asked Lanny as he saw me making for the door with my coat on.

"I'll be back by eight. Got a hot date, Weber fired up in the back yard."

"You could have two solid hours of live shots between now and eight, you know," said Jerry with a hint of disapproval.

"Do I ever know it," I said. "I wouldn't mind if I had nothing to say, it's fun spinning them when there's no thread. But unfortunately here I have quite a lot to say, in various different directions, and that's the last time I want to be on camera."

"Good thinking, Boss," said Lanny, shooing me out the door. "Have a burger for me."

Outside Hart, I hustled along 2nd Street with my head down, cell phone to my ear, to ward off press interest if possible. I looked up only when I had taken the left on C and was within twenty yards of my reserved parking space. A man was leaning against the passenger door, arms folded, looking the other way. I did a quick scan for camera crews and was delighted to see none. It's much easier to blow off the print reporters because they can't catch you on camera looking rude for blowing them off. I looked back down at the sidewalk and began speaking into the cell phone so I would look busy as well as hurried.

"I know that, Lanny," I said, raising my voice so my un-welcome guest would be sure to hear, "but this is complicated! We have to think about the other members, we have to consider the position of the chairman, and I can think of three or four reasons—"

Here I could tell from the pavement (imprint of bird's foot in concrete) that I was just a few steps from my car, so I said, "Hang on a sec, I'll be right with you," and looked up.

"Evening, Senator."

"Paulie! I was sure you would be a goddamn reporter. What do you know, boy?"

"Well, I feel a whole lot more like I do now than I did a while ago."

"And you're doubtless the better for it. Do you need a lift?"

"No, just an answer."

I looked into his face for a moment without saying any-thing. I slid the cell phone into my pocket. "So," I said. "Anson can't wait?"

Paulie nodded.

"Happy's been calling me too," I said.

"Happy's slicker'n a peeled onion, and he can do more push-ups for the ladies than a sagebrush lizard, but that hardly qualifies him."

"It's a funny town, Paulie. I'm still getting the hang of it. What you say is true, but one doesn't necessarily make the same decisions here as you would in, in your own life. At home, I mean."

"It's you that makes the decisions, Terry. The town doesn't make the decisions. You're the same guy you were in Boston, and Brooklyn."

"That's as may be," I said, moving around to the driver's side and putting the key in the lock. "I'll keep thinking about it, but now I've got to get to the house for dinner."

"Fair enough," said Paulie. "Just keep in mind: the only thing Anson Vivian has ever done behind his wife's back is zip her up."

"Fair enough." I laughed and hit the accelerator. In the

rearview mirror I noticed Paulie was wearing a necktie. No wonder he seemed different.

Sophisticated guy in a lot of ways, Paulie. Kind of misses the big picture sometimes, though.

IN GEORGETOWN, I WAS DISPLEASED to see an unfamiliar silver Volvo parked squarely in front of our gate. Worse, Emma was not on the stoop to greet me, must be inside receiving the visitor. If this is a reporter who thinks they're going to delay my cheeseburger in paradise, they'd better think twice. I kept the eucalyptus nut in my pocket to use as a weapon if need be, and pushed through the front door, which was ajar.

Emma was sitting in the living room, her hands on her knees, opposite a young woman in tears. I know this person, who is it?

"It's just that they all expect me to go out and perform like a trained seal," she blubbered, "but nobody ever trained me to be a seal, or anything else." She was having a hard time.

"I know, I know," said Emma. "It ain't easy. The main thing is to remember who you are, and don't let it roll you over, you know, crush you."

"If it was just me, it wouldn't be a problem, but it always gets to, well, you know. Daddy."

Oh. Josie Tillotson. Almost didn't recognize her without Happy Gilliam draped all over her.

"Hi, Josie. Sorry to intrude," I said and leaned over to give Emma a kiss.

Josie pulled herself together, touched a handkerchief to her eyes. "Not at all, Senator, I was just leaving, and your wonderful wife has been so kind. Thank you so much for the iced tea, Mrs. Mullally."

"Emma."

"Emma." She was out the door and into the Volvo without another word.

"I like that kid," said Emma. "She's almost my age, but she's a kid."

Emma was shaking with rage. I knew better than to launch into a conversation of any kind.

■

WHAT DID HAPPY IN was he couldn't let well enough alone. His putative opponent, Martha Holloway, was deep in an unsavory news trough, and he had to go change the subject to prove he could play hardball, too. He evidently couldn't stand seeing Holloway and Frobisch all alone on the high wire in the center ring.

At the opening of that evening's session—which we watched on the office TV, to see which way the wind was going to be blowing—Senator Harlan T. Gilliam of Texas rose on the floor of a thinly populated United States Senate to address what he said was a point of personal privilege. Thus he was able to interrupt debate.

"This better be good," said Lanny.

It wasn't.

Gilliam was sure his colleagues had all heard the ghastly news about the vice president evidently committing "illegal extortion"—nice touch, I thought—an offense punishable by twenty years' imprisonment under our great nation's criminal code.

Gilliam was personally acquainted with the victim of the crime, had been for many years—and for millions of dollars, I expected—and knew him to be a gentleman of the utmost integrity, whose word was beyond reproach.

"He's painting you into a corner, Boss," said Lanny. I nodded.

In a circumstance of this gravity, Gilliam went on, the Constitution of the United States imposes special obligations upon the elected members of the Congress. We cannot stand idly by. We must not shirk our responsibilities. We must swiftly convene and conduct hearings, hearings of law and hearings of fact, so as to expose to fresh air the conduct of the defendant individual, and if warranted by the law and the facts, to impeach and remove her from office. The members of Congress have a *fiduciary duty* to do no less."

He sat down to scattered applause from a few partisan Democrats on the floor, silence from the gallery.

"Whew!" Lanny blew out air.

Jerry was acerbic. "The press is going to feel like they have a fiduciary duty too, pal," she sneered to the TV set.

"What's that?" asked Bull Flannery.

"Fiduciary duty to tell the world, and particularly the Honorable Norbert Tillotson of McLean, Virginia, that his best friend, Senator Harlan Gilliam of Texas, has been busy screwing his twenty-five-year-old daughter."

"Do you think they have that story?" asked Bull Flannery. What a priceless straight man. Must make note to jack his salary, not that he's going anywhere.

Jerry snorted. "If they don't have it as we sit here, they will by tomorrow morning's editions."

JERRY KNEW HER BUSINESS. The next morning, the *Examiner,* the more conservative of the two Washington papers, ran a page-one exposé of the affair between Happy Gilliam and Josie Tillotson. No photos, but a few witness accounts of late-night hand-holding in hotels and the like, quoting "official sources." Even a reference to the weekend at Camp David, when the judge had to leave early. Bad enough, and it got worse.

Josie was only a prop. The paper made Gilliam—its long-time ally—look like a total hyena by detailing the political and personal relationship between him and his college classmate: former U.S. representative, now chief judge, Norbert Tillotson, head of the judicial panel that passes on the appointment of independent prosecutors under the Ethics in Government

Act of 1978. They had served in the House together, Gilliam had been a groomsman at Tillotson's wedding. (And Josie's horse race, I remembered.)

By artful juxtaposition—recent joint presence at the Silver Cup steeplechase, early departure from Camp David—the story suggested that Chief Judge Tillotson was well aware of his old friend's hold over his daughter, and that he would therefore feel obliged to toe Gilliam's line when it came to appointing independent prosecutors. This, it was suggested, represented a violation of his judicial oath. Pretty nasty.

Emma's features settled to stone as she read the piece, standing just inside the front door in her bathrobe.

"I'm going to go see her," she said.

"That would be a kindness. Try not to get in the day-two news story, though."

"*What!?*"

"I'm sorry, honey, you know what I mean. I think you're right to see her, forget what I said, I'm sorry."

I was sorry, too, all the way down Rock Creek Parkway. Sorry for Josie, and sorry I hadn't gotten out of the house before putting my foot in my mouth.

I called Emma from the office at ten.

"I found her at her mother's. She's, of course, not going anywhere, the place is staked out, all the networks, same at the courthouse, some cameras at her father's house, too, even though he's not there. Josie is completely destroyed, feels she's betrayed her father, not able to cope with it at all, and why should she be? Just keeps saying, Why did they bring Daddy in, why did they bring Daddy in? He didn't do anything, he didn't even know! She's not rational, it's all bound up with her guilt feelings about her parents' divorce. She thinks everything is her fault."

"Rough. Rough stuff."

"I know they slanted it against Tillotson because they don't like him, but where did they get the story? Have they been sitting on it, waiting for an excuse?"

"No, the *Examiner* would never sit on that story for five

minutes, too afraid they'd get burned. According to Jerry's moles, the story came from somewhere in the White House."

"So *they've* been sitting on it."

"Apparently so."

"Interesting town," said Emma.

"Wait 'til Friday if you want to see interesting."

"What's that?"

"Vivian has scheduled a Judiciary Committee hearing on the stuff against Holloway. Not an impeachment hearing, that would be up to the House at this point, but an oversight hearing into the operation of the Justice Department, and her role in it. Vivian's going to preside."

"Anson is as Anson does. This is where you're a witness?"

"I'm the only live witness. The rest is in the record, canned. Tom Fenster put in a written prima facie case, through background papers on the Agriculture Committee issues over the years, their economic impact, various people's positions on them, and a decade of Sam Burriss's dealings with 'Mattie' Holloway. Looks like a mountain of evidence, but if you know the law, none of it proves the extortion charge without the conversation at Camp David, the one when I was there."

"What are you going to say?"

"I never know 'til I open my mouth."

I did know one thing, though. I was going to bone up on every single page of Tom Fenster's materials, not just the executive summary, so I would know what facts I had to steer around, if it came to that. Any decent riverboat pilot knows the snags.

■

THERE WAS A KNOCK AT OUR DOOR on Olive Street at ten-thirty Wednesday evening. We don't have an intercom or a fish-eye—too New York, too high-rise—so I simply opened the door. I never do so without thinking of the case in Massachusetts where an executive was shot to death point-blank through his screen when he opened the door to an early-morning knock, but what are you going to do? We really are all helpless, if someone wants to do us in.

It was Phil Vacco. He had no raincoat, and had gotten soaked between his car and the porch. He didn't seem to notice this.

"Phil, you look a fright. Come on in." I gestured hospitably, but my heart was pounding. Which Phil Vacco was this going to be, the one who kept finding out more about Rudy Solano and Olie Wing, or the one who liked to talk about federal judgeships?

"No need, no need." He waved his hand. He stood just inside the screen door, propping it open with his leg. He was huffing and puffing, though I could see his car right there on Olive, the hood steaming in the rain.

"I've just come from the Observatory," he said. This meant the vice president's official residence.

"Phil, I want you and the vice president to know that I thought Happy Gilliam's attack on her was utterly reprehen—"

Phil held up his hand. "She knows that. She's only sorry that Happy dragged that poor girl and her father into this. I'm here on something else."

"Yes?"

"Friday is your turn on the griddle, and I want to be very clear that no matter what happens we're friends."

"Of course. That goes without—"

"I just want to, I need to make you aware of a couple of things." Phil was agitated, gesticulating, not his normal unflappable self.

"Oh, really? What's that?" I scraped a bit of loose paint off the side of the doorway with my finger.

I could feel throbbing in my chest.

"Number one, the Criminal Division has decided not to empanel a grand jury on any of those crappy little allegations about fund-raising at the Humphrey Center. We concur in your analysis: maybe embarrassing, but not heavy enough, and we won't take the cheap shot. Decision made at the Observatory tonight."

"Well, I certainly agree with and, and, appreciate that."

"Number two, the investigation on those commodity pools has been shut down. It never panned out, there was no there there. Just chitchat on the wire from outsiders trying to sound smart. Goes for you, goes for Happy Gilliam, too. Those cases are closed. You can tell him if you like, though of course not where you got the info."

"Of course." I guess they don't waste bullets by shooting men they've already killed. Happy was history, after Wednesday's papers.

"You're saving the stuff on Frobisch and the other two, the Tremblay stuff?"

Phil waved the question away. "Not currently relevant." Oh! Of course!

"Number three, on that New York and Hong Kong matter we were discussing the other day, Olie Wing has been picked up, arrested. A final decision was made to extradite him to the Chinese authorities for incarceration in China, as they desire. He is over the water as we speak. For your information, a determination has been made by the department that Wing is a pathological liar. He has been totally and officially discredited as an informant. We are giving the Chinese certain evidence we have developed here so they can hold him, and have let them know in no uncertain terms that his many stories are nothing but a patchwork of lies. He will be in solitary over there, no further debriefings."

Yes! My right hand tightened in a celebratory fist. I slid it behind me.

"In addition, that ancient-history investigation of police corruption in Manhattan and Brooklyn has been closed, anything we could have found would obviously be beyond the statute of limitations, and Solano is dead in any event. So, that's all gone. Not that it was ever anywhere in the first place."

I felt my heart lift. I nodded and smiled. Sure. Not that it was ever anywhere.

I thought of the ninety thousand dollars that Rudy Solano had handed me in 1989. My heartbeat now was like then. Wrongdoing is exciting. I thought of Rudy pitching in the snow in New Hampshire, sinking, like a drowning man, his blood eddying out around him. 1997.

I thought of my incredible naïveté and bad judgment in dealing with the lobbyists, the desire for ease that had led me to acquiesce for a time in Happy Gilliam's schemes, illegal fund-raising and illegal gratuities. Or worse. Both 1999. I had convicted people on less evidence.

I thought of a lot of questions that were not going to be asked of me now, were never going to be asked.

"Sure," I said. "Makes sense."

"All decisions were made at the veep level," said Phil. "She has oversight responsibility for Justice, as you know. She was all over these issues amazingly quickly. She's a real prosecutor's prosecutor."

"Sure. I know. I've always said that. Well, that's, that's, good to know." I extended my hand. Phil shook it and turned to go down the steps. Over his shoulder, he said, "This is purely informational. You don't have to forget it, but you should forget where you heard it."

"I understand," I said. "Good night. Good night, Phil. Say hi to Romy."

I closed the door, stood a moment with my eyes pressed shut.

What is Vivian offering me? He's not offering, he's only asking. I love what he represents, but we may never get to closure here, never get to mutual use.

Holloway, on the other hand, has offered and has just delivered. And it may not end there. The lady seems to understand hardball and softball.

I climbed the stairs to Emma, warm in our bed. Life was good. Life was suddenly very much better.

■

EMMA SHOOK ME AWAKE AT 4:00 A.M. on Friday morning.
"I can't stand your tossing and turning anymore," she said.
"Let's go walk on the towpath, maybe you can spit out what
ails you."

This was the best idea I'd heard since the all-night drive to
Big Ugly. Within minutes, we had passed the last of the M
Street carousers and dropped down past the old railroad right-
of-way to the canal. At this hour, there were no bicyclists to
spoil our favorite escape in Washington. A gibbous moon made
the going easy.

"Fastest way to get out of town I know," said Emma as she
tiptoed off balance along a spillway with a few inches of water
on it.

We stopped on the spillway and studied the canal. "Somehow, I don't have quite the same urge to jump in here as I usually do with fresh water," said Emma.

The near and far bank were covered with mud and leaves,
while the entire middle section of the canal was choked with
lime-green weeds, waving in the current, reaching almost to
the surface. I thought of a story Paulie Kovalla had told us
about a West Virginia woman who had been murdered by her
husband and dumped in a lake. Her body was found years later
in an ice-cold underwater cave only because her beautiful hair
grew to four feet, and waved enough to attract the attention of
a diver.

"I'm with you," I said. "You go in there, you'd expect to
encounter something real soon."

Emma read my mind. "Like, a body."

"Those weeds look like a woman's hair."

"I could tell you were repelled by that story of Paulie's. I
could see it going 'plunk!' into your little memory box, rattling
around in there until it needed to be dredged up."

"Sweet, let me ask you something: What's the sense of me being a human being, postchimpanzee and even postbonobo, lots of gray matter, forehead straight up and down, if you know what I'm thinking before I even say it?"

Emma ran her fingers through my hair, mussing my part and making everything stick up and out. "I don't need you to be a *Homo sapiens*," she said. "I'd be perfectly content if you were a tree." This was an amatory advance.

"If you were a locust tree, I could stick pennies in your bark." She poked me in the ribs.

"That would tickle. Maybe I will become a locust tree."

"One other thing, whatever you had to drink last night when you were downstairs by yourself? You should have it every night."

I had had nothing to drink, but I kept that to myself. I put my arm around her shoulder.

After a mile's walk, we came to the shed where during the day they sell Cokes and rudimentary fishing gear—bobbers, hand lines, nothing fancy. We left the towpath and crossed a small stream to hit the trail leading to the Potomac.

It's only a few hundred yards to the river, but there are more twists and turns in the landscape than you can shake a stick at: from northeast hardwood forest to sand and Cape Cod scrub, to granite outcroppings and blueberry bushes. For vegetation and topography, Washington, D.C., is a paradise. We followed the trail to the end and climbed through dense brush to reach a series of smooth rocks, a promontory into the river. Here we sat. Emma took off her sopping-wet sneakers, wiggled her toes in the water.

"That is something I would not do for all the tea in China," I observed.

She leaned over and mussed my hair again. I hate that, and she knows it. "Yes, I know, beset as you are by boyhood memories of mean snapping turtles . . ."

"Beset as I am."

Emma was aware I would not be able to concentrate as

long as her toes remained in the danger zone, so she withdrew them to safety, clasped her knees to her chin, and gave me a sideways look. "You were tossing and turning," she reminded.

Yes, I had been tossing and turning in our bed, after falling deeply asleep. I had dreamed yet again of being a prisoner in the dock, this time being lectured by Judge Harlan Gilliam and Judge Anson Vivian, both wearing long black nighties.

Here, however, the rock bass were breaking water in the current twenty feet from me, while the first sun was beginning to pick out the tips of the hardwoods on top of the bluff opposite. Emma had been right to bring us to this spot.

"It's just that I have a lot on my plate. I have to testify tomorrow, and that could go any which way, even though I have today to prepare, and soon I've got to decide whether to support Vivian for 2000. On top of all that, Phil Vacco has been helpful on a number of fronts, and says the VP is a big fan of ours, you and me both. So the whole thing is just a mess, a hodgepodge."

Emma looked straight ahead, at the river. "So why were you tossing and turning? It's fairly clear what you have to do."

A rock bass jumped out of water so close to shore I could have reached it with a net. I put my arm around Emma again.

"You're right," I said. "In this light, it's clear."

■

A<small>T</small> 10:00 A.M. ON FRIDAY, JULY 30, 1999, the sergeant-at-arms of the United States Senate was draped in gold braid as he banged his staff on the floor to open the morning session of the Committee on the Judiciary. It could not have been more obvious that all the rules of parliamentary procedure, of due process, of protocol, and of senatorial courtesy were to be punctiliously observed.

Senator Anson Vivian of West Virginia assumed the chair. He explained that his esteemed colleague, Senator Gilliam of Texas, who had requested this hearing, had been obliged to return to his native state to attend to pressing business, a town-wide meeting in Piscapadula.

I leaned over to Lanny. "Where's that?" I whispered.

"Panhandle," he whispered back, covering his mouth with his hand. "Million miles from nowhere. Population maybe sixty. No TV, is what they're hoping. Good luck. The networks will all rent choppers. Lyndon Johnson started that in the 'forty-eight Senate campaign." I nodded. The tragedy of Lanny Green is he was born thirty years too late to be on *The $64,000 Question* TV show.

Senator Vivian's eyes twinkled as I asked to be sworn. I smiled right back at him. Being sworn was optional for members, but I wanted no mistaking my intentions.

Seated at a table to the side, without a lawyer, and staring not at me but at Anson Vivian, was the vice president of the United States, Martha Holloway, from time to time chewing on her glasses. Seated well into the crowd behind her was the Honorable Philip Vacco, assistant attorney general in charge of the Criminal Division, U.S. Department of Justice.

The majority counsel for the committee, a handsome young man named Eric Prince, rose to his full height of five and a half feet, buttoned and unbuttoned his middle button a few times, and cleared his throat. He seemed aware he was auditioning for a position as United States Senator, or at least federal district judge.

"Mr. Chairman," he squeaked in a voice devoid of experience, a voice only dogs could hear clearly, "the members of the committee will no doubt have in mind the written submission by counsel for Mr. Burriss, the legislative agent for American agricultural interests, and member of the District of Columbia bar." All I could think was, air traffic controllers can tell when a pilot gets in trouble: his voice rises at least an octave. Wait, what was Mr. Prince saying?

"The evidence will demonstrate that the vice president of

the United States, at her Camp David office and in her official capacity, made to him certain statements which have become the subject of an official criminal investigation under the federal extortion and racketeering statutes, namely 18 U.S. Code Section 1951, the Hobbs Act, a felony carrying a term of up to twenty years imprisonment, and 18 U.S. Code Sections 1961 and following, the so-called RICO statute, also a twenty-year felony."

I looked at Holloway. She kept on chewing, didn't look at me, looked at Vivian.

"The members of the committee will also have in mind that as Attorney Burriss has noted, a number of the statements made by Vice President Holloway occurred in the presence of a witness, namely United States Senator Terrence Mullally of Massachusetts, who is here this morning and who is in a position to be able to corroborate the statement of Mr. Burriss."

The majority leader and committee chairman welcomed me, thanked me in advance. I smiled and nodded. I was in a position, after all. What else should I do but smile and nod? Go with the flow, unless and until you have to make your break. That way you get a few steps head start, while people are reacting. Ask anyone who's been a prisoner, who's tried to escape.

"You may proceed," said Vivian.

Prince cleared his throat again. His voice broke as he asked me to state my name for the record.

"Terrence Mullally, no middle initial."

"Your occupation, sir?"

"United States Senator."

"You are familiar with the written record of evidence adduced in this case?"

"I glanced through it, yes." Prince smiled. This was going to be easier than he had thought. He had an unprepared witness.

"Would you agree with me, sir, that the record demonstrates a lengthy course of dealing between Mr. Samuel Burriss, as the registered agent for certain agricultural interests, and the vice president of the United States acting in her official capacity?"

"Yes, I certainly would."

"You have no reason to dispute that Mr. Burriss since the beginning of this administration has advocated his clients' position before the vice president in her official capacity?"

"None at all. Nothing the matter with that."

Prince frowned at my editorial. "Thank you. Just answer the question yes or no, please, Senator.

"So, the evidence shows a pattern of dealing between Mr. Burriss and the defendant, Ms. Holloway?"

"She is not a defendant here."

"Between Mr. Burriss and Ms. Holloway?"

"Yes, that is fair, a pattern. Yes."

Prince was well pleased with this. Acting under color of office and a pattern of activity are key elements of the charge under the extortion and racketeering statutes.

But Prince was forgetting what he knew before he went to law school: you need some ham in the sandwich if you're going to call it a ham sandwich. Doesn't matter what the law is unless you've got the facts.

"You were a federal prosecutor for many years, sir?"

"For seven years."

"You have personally tried extortion and racketeering cases?"

"Eight or ten, yes."

"It is the law, is it not, that a single unlawful act may be sufficient to prove a course and pattern of dealing was illegal?"

"That is the law, yes."

Prince took off his glasses and walked up to me, like Perry Mason. "Now, sir, directing your attention to the afternoon of July 25, 1999, were you a guest of the vice president's at Camp David?"

"My wife and I were, yes." Never mind that Emma had already left for Johns Hopkins by then: we don't need any extraneous issues cluttering up what's about to happen.

"And were you present at a conversation between Mr. Samuel Burriss and Vice President Holloway, occurring in her official study there, following luncheon on Sunday?"

"I was."

"You are in a position to confirm what was said between the two of them?"

"I am."

"The discussion concerned two topics, did it not, the administration's price supports bill and the vice president's Everglades bill?"

"That is correct."

I looked up at Vivian. He had a thumb and two fingers in his mouth. Unlike Prince, he didn't look at all exultant. Anson's been around the block a few times, I thought. He knows this is too easy.

"And would you tell us, sir, the conversation on those two topics, what was said by her and what was said by him."

"Certainly. He said, 'If you don't switch your position on price supports, you'll be sorry, Mattie. I'll make sure you're sorry.' He called her Mattie. I had not known that was a nickname of the vice president. And he stressed the word 'sorry.'"

"What? What else did he say?"

"He said he would see to it that thirty million dollars would be raised against her if she ran for president in 2000, unless she changed her position on price supports."

"You have read the written submissions, Senator. Did he not say that her legislation would *cost* his clients thirty million dollars a year?"

"I know that's what it says in there, and possibly Sam, who is a good man, one of the great ones, in fact—and I *agree* with him on the issue, by the way—got confused in the heat of the conversation, but that's not quite how it happened, not what was said, anyway. Actually, if you look at Tab Eleven of the written submission—" I pointed to the briefing book in front of Prince, who obediently turned to Tab Eleven—"you'll see computations by the agribusiness industry showing that the actual cost to them would be over a hundred million dollars a year. Thirty million dollars is the cost of a presidential campaign, if the candidate accepts public funding after the primary. It's not the cost of this legislation they were discussing."

Prince ran his finger along the columns of figures at Tab

Eleven, looking for help. But they footed to a hundred and seven million dollars, in his copy as in mine. *Be careful what you ask for.* He looked up at me in exasperation.

"You have read the statement by Mr. Burriss, sir. Did the vice president not say she would *crush* his clients unless they withdrew their opposition to her Everglades bill?"

"No, she said, 'Sam, I know your clients want to clear-cut the Everglades, but I am *crushed* you would stoop to threatening me. I simply will not operate with a gun to my head. I know all about guns,' which I guess she does."

Vice President Holloway stopped chewing on the stem of her glasses and gave a sour, almost imperceptible, nod in confirmation of my account. No jubilation. Just exasperation. That's what happened, why are we here? Her right hand began drumming.

The room was in pandemonium. Senators were ducking out as fast as they could, Republicans and Democrats both. Anson Vivian gaveled the hearings to a close *sine die*, announced the Senate was in its August recess. No sense protracting that disaster on national television. He caught my eye and smiled at me before disappearing into the back room. Anson is a man of style. Perhaps he really is more interested in dominion over land than in dominion over men.

I looked around and found Emma in the crowd, standing with Lanny. She pretended to be adjusting the fabric on the shoulder of her dress, but was actually giving me a thumbs-up sign. Phil Vacco walked over to join them, shook both their hands rather formally.

The media mobbed Vice President Holloway. Needlessly: she was going exactly nowhere. She had all day, all year for this. She stood to face the mikes, and with dignity and humor confirmed my account in every particular while I was making my way to the back of the room.

Emma gave me a quick kiss.

"Why the thumbs up?" I whispered.

"Because," she whispered back, "you woke up, you big sleepyhead."

EPILOGUE

I GUESS YOU KNOW THE REST.

On Tuesday, August 3, the Justice Department announced that its criminal investigation of Vice President Holloway had been "suspended."

Two days after that, Myron Brinker, back in Washington, announced he would not after all be a candidate for the Republican presidential nomination in 2000. I offered to bet Lanny a nickel that the Criminal Division's investigation of Attorney General Frobisch had recently been closed, but he wouldn't take the wager.

Happy Gilliam resigned his seat, went home, and never left Texas again. His wife seemed relieved, and joined him there.

Anson Vivian, underfunded but gallant, soldiered on throughout the fall and winter. I officially endorsed him the week before the New Hampshire primary—I knew Martha Holloway would understand I had to preserve my options— but the move against the vice president had flunked the ha-ha test. The perceived phoniness of the allegations clung to Vivian like a burr.

In January, the populist Democratic governor of North Dakota, Ed Matthiesson, got into the race; his platform was a vow not to set foot in Washington, D.C., until his inauguration. He lost New Hampshire to Vivian—something about those mountains—but beat him head to head in South Carolina and Washington State, and in early March knocked him out of the race in California and New York.

Matthiesson had even less money than Vivian, as the Democratic regulars looked down on him, but he wouldn't have won anyway. The country had basically made its choice the previous year: Martha Holloway had stood up, and had been counted. And so on November 7, 2000, by an electoral college margin of 493 to 45, she became the first woman elected president of the United States. Matthiesson carried only nine states: Alaska, Hawaii, Maine, Minnesota, Montana, North Dakota, Rhode Island, South Dakota, and Washington. (The District of Columbia, with three electoral votes, was apparently insulted by his campaign pledge.)

Emma and I watched the returns at the Humphrey Center, together with Lanny and Jerry and a gaggle of other Democratic senators and their wives—and in two cases, I'm happy to say, husbands.

The mood was upbeat, partly because most of the insiders didn't care for Matthiesson, and partly because the Democrats had extended our margin in the Senate from four seats to eight.

Still, we had lost the presidential election, so I had to pull a long face when they stuck the mike in front of me outside the building. I cleared my throat portentously and resolved to be as boring as I possibly could. This was not a story I wanted to be in.

"While President-Elect Holloway and I are of opposite political parties and do not agree on a number of issues, we all of course must and do respect the process. As Americans," I added, nodding again, in agreement with myself.

My interviewer was satisfied, shook the mike to signify a wrap, and the cameraman clicked off the klieg light. Darkness was never so sweet. I had survived the news cycle, once again.

As my eyes adjusted, I saw Lanny standing at the low stone wall with a blank expression and folded arms. It was a pity I would not be able to share with him the answer I had wanted to give to the camera:

While President-Elect Holloway and I are of opposite political parties and do not agree on a number of issues, I was actually pleased to have had some small role in bringing this result about.

Even if I had to shade the truth quite a bit to do it.

After all, I had preserved my options. Maybe I had sold a

couple of guys down the river, but they were no blood kin of mine. They were two mango leaves, where I had stashed the extra salt until they dropped off. Simple triage. After many false starts, I had finally got this place figured out. Situation covered.

As a result, I could still aspire to the highest offices in the land.